Penny Pecorelli has published many articles and short stories over the years and has broadcast on the radio. She lives in England with her Italian husband, but they have a house in Arezzo, Tuscany, which they and their family visit frequently and serves as the setting of this novel. Penny is passionate about the culture and traditions of Italy. This is her second novel. The first, *A Village in Time,* was set in the small hillside village in the south of Italy where her husband was born.

For Teresa and Luciano, and, of course, Giuseppe.

Penny Pecorelli

A Castle in Italy

AUSTIN MACAULEY PUBLISHERS™

LONDON ∗ CAMBRIDGE ∗ NEW YORK ∗ SHARJAH

A CIP catalogue record for this title is available from the British Library.

ISBN 9781035867943 (Paperback)
ISBN 9781035867950 (ePub e-book)

www.austinmacauley.com

First Published 2024
Austin Macauley Publishers Ltd®
1 Canada Square
Canary Wharf
London
E14 5AA

Thank you to my family, and of course the friends and relations in Arezzo who inspired this book.

Prequel

What do you do, Gabriella thought, if you are convinced you might have just met the love of your life and then he disappeared?

It had been quite extraordinary.

She and her friend Flick had been sitting on the tube in London, on their way to a lecture. They were chatting in a very desultory way when Flick suddenly said, "What's your ideal man? I mean what type would you pick?"

"Oh, I don't know," Gabriella laughed. She glanced around the packed carriage and her eyes lighted on a young man sitting in the far corner. On an impulse, she said, "Perhaps someone like that."

To her great embarrassment, he looked up in amusement. She must have spoken more loudly than she intended.

Their eyes met and it was incredible. She almost gasped at the shock of it. It was as if she had recognised him. Yet she had never seen him before in her life. Tall and wiry, hazel eyes, dark blonde hair.

He smiled at her and she couldn't help it. She smiled back. Her heart was pounding. They held each other's gaze for a long moment. She was dimly aware of Flick sitting next to her.

"Oh my god!" she heard Flick say. "It can't be true. You've just clicked! I've heard of instant attraction but this is ridiculous."

The train lurched to a stop and the young man got up. He passed them, glancing down at her as he did so.

Then he was gone.

But so was Flick.

"Catch up with you later," Flick called as she dived off the train.

Gabriella was stunned. Where was Flick going? Surely, not after him?

She couldn't believe what was happening.

She got off the train several stops later and stumbled into class. There was no way she could concentrate on a lecture on accounting after that meeting on the train. His image kept flashing into her mind. And what was Flick doing? Was she asking him for his number? Giving him hers? She didn't usually respond to pickups but somehow this was different. She was half hoping that Flick wasn't embarrassing herself and her by asking for his number but the other half of her was desperate to see him again and hoping that she was.

Flick appeared in the canteen at lunchtime. She was grinning.

"Where did you go?" Gabriella demanded. She hoped she knew the answer.

"I found him. Gave him your phone number."

"You didn't!" Gabriella protested. But secretly she was thrilled.

"I think he was pleased."

"He's probably married or engaged or something."

"No ring. I checked."

"Not all men wear rings," Gabriella replied.

"No, but he didn't look married. Anyway we'll just have to wait and see, won't we?" Flick said smugly.

"I don't know whether to hug you or never speak to you again," Gabriella said.

"Oh, I think you need to hug me. When I caught up with him, he had already turned to come back into the carriage to get your number. I've never seen anyone so relieved to see me. I think he thought he had lost his chance." :

But what happened next changed everything.

Chapter 1

When the phone rings in the middle of the night, it's rarely good news.

"It's your father, Gabriella."

It was Antonio, her father's right-hand man for as long as Gabriella could remember.

His voice was quivering with strong emotion. "He's had a stroke. You need to come, come now. As quickly as you can. It's bad. Very bad."

"Is he…?" Her voice broke.

"He's still alive and the doctor is with him."

She had thrown on a pair of jeans, a sweater and a jacket, pushed some things into a bag, grabbed her passport and handbag, then woken Flick in the next room to tell her she had to go and to explain to the lecturers what had happened.

She raced to the airport and was lucky enough to get a flight to Florence within the hour. She had phoned ahead and Tommaso, her father's driver was waiting for her as she landed, his face grave.

"Is he…?" She stuttered.

"Still alive. I have just telephoned."

"Hurry, Tommaso, hurry," she said.

They had raced along the autostrada, turning off after three-quarters of an hour to take the winding road to Marinella. Despite her panic, there had been a thrill of excitement and recognition as they sped through the high gates and up the long avenue lined with tall, dark cypress trees and past the fields of the vast estate.

They crunched to a skidding halt and a swirl of gravel at the front door of the Castello. Built in the twelfth century to withstand marauding tribes, its sturdy stone walls and crenelated towers were like something out of a fairy tale.

Except it was real and it was her home. She had lived there since she was born, her mother having died giving birth to her.

Carmela, Antonio's wife, had flung open the front door when she heard the car. No time for hugs of welcome; Gabriella was out of the car before it had quite stopped, was up the steps, into the hall and up the wide staircase, taking the stairs two at a time.

It seemed that the room where her father lay had been full of people. The doctor, two nurses, Antonio, even the count's favourite hound Lupo lying in the corner…but there was only one person that mattered.

She flung herself down at her father's bedside and grasped his hand. "Papa," she whispered, "I am here."

"Gabriella, carissima." She could only just hear him.

Then there was the faintest of sighs.

It had taken her a moment to realise, then, "Papa!" she had screamed.

The doctor had moved swiftly to the bedside and held her father's wrist before bending his head to listen to his chest.

He had stood in silence for a moment, his head bowed, before turning to Gabriella and saying, "I am afraid he has gone. I am so sorry. He waited only for you."

And dimly, Gabriella could hear the count's dog Lupo begin to howl in grief as if he too knew his loss.

So from that moment, Contessa Gabriella Teresa Maria di Valdarno was an orphan.

Chapter 2

The next few weeks seemed endless, her mind moving seemingly through a thick fog of unreality. There was only one solid fact that recurred to her again and again and that was the dawning realisation that her carefree youth as a student in London had come to an abrupt end. It wasn't supposed to be like this. Her father was meant to have lived forever; she was to have finished her degree and forged a career before one day, perhaps in the very distant future, coming home to take charge of the estate.

It was all too soon, much too soon, and mingled with the grief she felt for her father was rage; rage that fate had dealt her such a cruel blow.

The funeral, as was the custom in Italy, had been very quick. Forty-eight hours after the death of the count in fact.

The ancient family chapel on the estate amidst the vineyards had been deemed too small to hold the number of people they were expecting so it was swiftly organised in the Duomo, the cathedral in Arezzo, the nearby city. She was glad that the avuncular bishop took charge as he could see her distress, advising her on the mass and details of the service as she had never had to arrange a funeral before.

Aged family members from all parts of Italy and in fact the wider world, had rushed to be there. She had no very close relatives but old uncles and aunts by marriage, cousins, plus the great and the good from the surrounding area, all wanted to embrace her, to offer her consolation and advice. The Duomo was a sea of black, only the bishop's white robes relieving the gloom. Representatives of the charities of which he had been patron, stood rigidly to attention alongside the coffin.

It had been torture standing after the long mass as was the custom, to shake hands and occasionally receive kisses and embraces from an endless queue of people, most of whom she barely knew. Among them, crying crocodile tears and fawning over her was Domenico, a distant cousin who had been trying for years to persuade her to marry him, presumably in the hope of inheriting the Castello and the money he believed went with it.

With him was his equally unsavoury mother, Cara, who had tried, also unsuccessfully, to ingratiate herself with the count. The thought of this woman as her stepmother had made her flesh creep. Her father, however, had remained faithful to the memory of Gabriella's mother and no woman, least of all Cara, could ever measure up to her.

The only consolation Gabriella had taken from the service had been the presence of the estate staff: Carmela and Antonio, the husband and wife team who had almost been like parents to her, Rosanna, her old nanny, Tommaso, her father's driver, and the dozens of workers on the land who were genuinely grief-stricken. There were also many local villagers who had come to pay their respects, sitting timidly at the back of the Duomo, in their ill-fitting clothes, overawed by the grandeur of the building and of the occasion. At least they were sincere in their grief because she knew her father had been loved and respected by them all.

At last, it was all over and she could return to the Castello, retire and give vent to her feelings, uttering a silent scream of agony to the four walls of her bedroom.

But there was also fear, an overwhelming sense of fear at what the future now held for her. Lupo curled in the corner of the room where he had taken to sleeping since his master's death, padded over to her and she clung to him for comfort.

****

In the days that followed, Rosanna helped her sort out her father's many possessions and his clothes, most of which they bundled up for charity. She did offer some to Antonio and Tommaso and after a little persuading, they both took a few of his sweaters.

"To remember him by," Antonio said, smoothing the soft wool. Tommaso also took a jacket and a pair of stout boots.

She and Rosanna wept as they emptied the wardrobes and drawers of years of clothes and other objects. He had always been a tidy man but they found tucked away many mementoes of his wife, Gabriella's mother; photos, a lock of her hair in a little silver box and her wedding and engagement rings. These of course had always been intended to be left to Gabriella and she stored them away safely. She also kept his favourite sweater to wrap herself in. It still contained a faint aroma of him and she buried her face in it. The photo of her parents' wedding day when they looked so young and hopeful and radiant with love, not realising the tragedy that lay ahead, she also transferred to her own dressing table, together with other albums of family photos.

Finally, it was all done and she and Rosanna clung together in grief, realising that all trace of him would now be gone from the room he had slept in since he was born and where he had died, too young. She could only hope that somewhere, somehow he was reunited with the wife he had adored.

There had of course also been the reading of the will, the formal meeting in the solicitor's office, the old family lawyer who had been a friend of the count's for many years and who tried to sound official but whose voice cracked on occasion as he glanced at Gabriella sitting stern-faced trying to keep her emotions in check. She was flanked by Antonio, Carmela, Rosanna, and Tommaso whom she had asked to accompany her.

The bulk of the estate was of course left to her, but there were other bequests, a sum of money to each of the four people sitting close to her in recognition of their long and faithful service. There was a special mention of thanks for the care and devotion Carmela and Rosanna had given to Gabriella herself since the death of his beloved wife. Gabriella heard a scarcely suppressed sob from Carmela, and glancing at the pair of them, she saw tears in the eyes of both women.

To Antonio, he had bequeathed his watch, a family heirloom which had been passed down through several generations. He too was struggling to control his emotions and Carmela gave his hand a comforting squeeze. Then several valuable guns were left to Tommaso and he also wiped a tear from his eye. The count had also stipulated that they had a home for life on the estate.

This last provision made Gabriella suddenly realise with a shock how important it was for her to keep hold of the Castello and the estate or losing it might make the four of them homeless. She shivered in fear.

When the formalities were over, the solicitor came forward and shook the hands of the four of them and then, finally, turning to Gabriella, he hesitated, uncertain whether it would be correct to embrace her. She, seeing his dilemma, moved forward and embraced him, thanking him for his years of service to the family.

"I am always here to support you, Gabriella," he said, releasing her. "Any advice you ever need, just ring me. Your father was a good man and held his position lightly. He did his best for everyone and there are not many of such rank who do."

"Thank you," Gabriella said. "I am so grateful."

She couldn't be sure but as they left the solicitor's office, she saw a figure lurking in the shadows of a nearby building and she was almost certain it was her cousin Domenico, watching and waiting.

After such an episode of high emotion, she took them all out to lunch at a nearby trattoria. Soon reminiscences flowed and there was even some subdued laughter at a few of the memories they shared of past times and Gabriella could only be grateful for the affection and feeling of warmth and support they all gave her.

Chapter 3

But now the work had to begin.

The estate, the staff of thirty who worked in the Castello and in the grounds; the domestics, the vintners, those who looked after the olives and the gardens. They were all her responsibility now. She had lain for a moment, rigid in her bed, a sense of terror sweeping over her, paralysing her. She was only twenty-three, a time when she should have been out partying, enjoying herself. Why had God done this to her? And her father, why had he left her in this mess?

But she wasn't her father's daughter for nothing. Slowly, though, the panic subsided and determination took over. Her father had brought her up to be fearless, not afraid of challenges: to face them and deal with them. And deal with them she must, whatever it took. She embraced Lupo who licked her face as if in support and patiently waited while she rose from her bed, splashed her face with water, dressed and went downstairs; Lupo followed her closely as if afraid to let her out of his sight.

The smell of coffee had come from the kitchen. It had always been her refuge in times of stress and there was the comforting, plump figure of Carmela who was in charge of the kitchen and already at work, her strong capable hands peeling and chopping vegetables with practised speed. Gabriella made her own coffee in the old-fashioned way with the little screw-topped coffee maker on the stove. Carmela had wanted to do it for her but Gabriella smiled and said she could manage.

"I haven't been a student for nearly three years without learning to fend for myself," she smiled.

One of the first things she had to do, she knew, was summon all the staff together and reassure them about the future. They must all be worried as to what was going to happen to them now. So she asked Antonio to gather everyone for a meeting.

Before they came, she walked up the steep stone steps of the tower with him to the highest point of the Castello on the crenelated terrace roof. It had always been her favourite spot where she had stood many times with her father gazing out at the several hundred acres of the estate to the wooded foothills of the Apennines beyond, those mountains which form the backbone of Italy.

Now it was Antonio who stood with her, looking down the valley at the old, gnarled olive trees, dating back, some of them, hundreds of years. On the lower slopes of the hills were the acres of vines with grapes ripening in the sun. Even nearer to the Castello were carpets of gold, the sunflowers just beginning to show their colour as they turned their heads to the sun.

Then, to one side of them were the kitchen gardens which provided vegetables for the house. There were also huts and runs for chickens and ducks which gave them fresh eggs every day. Last but not least were the elegant formal gardens laid out in the traditional patterns that had existed for centuries, the soft stone, the low clipped box hedges laid out in a geometric design, the elaborate flowing fountain in the centre with its statue of Aphrodite, the secret grotto inspired by the cloisters of medieval monasteries where she had sat giggling with friends as a teenager, tucked away from prying adult eyes; the vine-covered pergola, the terracotta flagstones. There were, as was traditional in Italian gardens, very few flowers but the cascading bright pink bougainvillea near the entrance of the Castello broke all the rules. On the terrace, scented jasmine and tubs of herbs were placed in spots where the visitor could brush against them and release their fragrance. Antique statues were dotted around in the corners amid pots of lemon trees.

All wonderful but all required so much work and expense and so many staff to maintain them.

A silence filled them both. Antonio was a man approaching his sixty-fifth year, grey-haired and weatherbeaten and tough as only a man could be who had spent his whole life working outdoors. They gazed together at the scene before them, at the land they would both die for, as many had done before in war and toil.

Gabriella broke the silence at last.

"First of all, Antonio," she began, "I want to thank you for all the years you have given to my father. I know he loved and respected you like a brother and I would be very honoured if you would continue to help me. I don't know what the future holds but I want you to know I will do my very best to keep everything together here. Times are tough now in Italy, I know, but I will try. In case you were wondering, there is no question of me going back to England. That part of my life is finished. I know all the staff here will be very worried as to what is going to happen to them, but I will do my utmost to look after them all, with your help, and I want to reassure them of that."

She had been gazing out at the scene before her as she spoke, but now she turned to look at him and there were tears in his eyes. "Oh, Antonio, I know you loved him like a brother too and you will miss him as much as I will. You have always been like a second father to me."

"Thank you, Gabriella, for your kind words," he choked, his voice filled with emotion, "and you know I will do everything I can to help you. You are right, I was devoted to your father and was honoured to think he considered me like a brother."

"Now," she continued, "you must tell me everything that has been happening here. I need to get to grip with the finances."

She had realised with a shock that money wasn't anything she had ever really taken seriously, thinking it would always be there, in an endless pot. How out of touch she had been, how very spoilt. It had never occurred to her that things might be difficult, that her father might have been worried about how to keep the estate going and pay all the many staff.

There had been a pause and then the news that she had been half dreading had come. Antonio confirmed all her suspicions.

"Not good, I'm afraid. We tick along and the estate just about supports itself, but the oil and wine sales aren't as strong as they could be and I can't see much improvement in the near future." He paused and then said, "I think the main problem is the high cost of keeping up the Castello itself with constant repairs and maintenance. Each year another tower crumbles or a window needs replacing and all these things need specialist workers who are expensive. I have to say your father was worried about keeping his head above water." He hesitated, then added, "I think the worry must possibly have been one of the causes of his stroke."

Again Gabriella felt guilt-ridden. She had known none of this, far away in England enjoying her carefree life as a student where her biggest worry had only been to hand in an essay on time.

"We will have to go into the finances more carefully. Do you have any suggestions?" She said hopefully.

"I don't know what to say." He looked at her apologetically. "Tending the vines, making wine and oil, running the estate, that is all I have ever known."

There was a further, heavy silence.

"Maybe we could sell some of the land?" He suggested finally.

"If it comes to that." She didn't like the idea of it but she had to consider every possibility. There were also a number of very valuable antiques in the house but selling them would just be a drop in the ocean compared with what was needed.

"We are so lucky here, to have all this," she said slowly. "People would sell their souls to be part of it." She gazed down once more at the idyllic vista before her. An idea was slowly forming in her brain. What was Tuscany famous for?

Tourism, that was it. Every time anyone in England had asked where she had come from, they had always said how lucky she was that Italy and in particular, Tuscany, was famous for its food, its wine and above all for the beauty of its landscape.

They had a fabulous medieval castle, situated in one of the very best regions of Italy, if not the world, near the historic city of Arezzo and not that far from Florence and Siena with hundreds of other places of art, history and tradition within reach. It was, as everyone said, a region famed for its food and wine. They had so much to offer including their own oil and wine.

"Antonio," she said at last. "What would you say if I suggested that we turn this place into a hotel?"

There had been a stunned silence.

"Never let it be said," he replied eventually, "that you can't teach an old dog new tricks. If it means preserving all this, I am willing to learn."

She had flung her arms around him. "Thank you. Thank you so much."

He had disengaged himself awkwardly. "You are your father's daughter, that's for sure," he said, "where everyone else saw problems, he only saw opportunities. I know you will make a success of whatever you set out to do, but," he said cautiously, "you will need help. You will need someone by your side who knows the hotel business. I don't think it is as easy as all that to open your house to strangers. There are so many pitfalls and so many rules and regulations. You must get someone with accounting skills, someone with a background in hotel work, someone to support you."

"Yes, I agree," Gabriella replied, "but who?"

Who indeed?

Chapter 4

The meeting with the staff had gone ahead as planned. She reassured them that she would do her very best to look after them all and while most looked relieved others looked sceptical as if they privately wondered how a twenty-three-year-old student with no work experience would be able to cope with such a vast estate.

For now, she revealed nothing of her plans to turn the Castello into a hotel. They would have to be thought about very carefully.

Carmela in the kitchen for example. It was one thing to cook for a family, the staff and a few visitors, but a hotel full of people?

And the bedrooms! Those on the main floors had private bathrooms, but many on the upper floors did not, having shared bathrooms at the end of the corridors. She would have to convert the attic rooms for herself, a future manager, and any other live-in staff. And the plumbing was antiquated, not exactly medieval but given to breaking down when demand was at its height. They could still produce wine of course, and olive oil, and one of their best selling points would be fresh produce from the garden and fresh eggs from the hens and ducks but as Antonio had pointed out, the economy was not as strong as it could be.

Was she mad to even think of such a wild scheme?

No, she thought, I must have faith. It is the only way to keep this wonderful place. She thought of houses that she had visited in England, stately homes that had been the preserve of rich families, now handed over to the National Trust, opened to the public to wander round at will.

She sighed. It would all boil down to one thing.

Money: and lots of it. Without that, her plan would be impossible.

She would have to approach the bank for an overdraft.

Giovanni Batista, the bank manager was another old friend of her father's but she knew that in business, she couldn't rely on friendship. She had to convince him, be confident enough to show him that she was serious, that she could make a go of things.

She set to work drawing up plans, getting quotations from local builders, walking endlessly from top to toe of the Castello and trying to visualise what she would need.

Quite a few weeks later, she rang and made an appointment.

She was trying not to tremble as she opened the door of his office and walked in with a bright smile that belied her nerves. He rose from behind his large and imposing desk, came forward and kissed her politely on both cheeks, offering first of all his condolences on her father's death. Then he indicated a chair and she sat down.

He asked her about her life in London and when she hoped to return.

Then it was time for the pleasantries to be over.

She took a deep breath. "I am not going back. I am staying here. My duty is to the Castello and those who have worked there, giving loyal service to my father over many years, some of them for a very long time."

"Ah," he said, "and you have come to see me exactly why?"

At last, they were getting to the point. She had gone through the books very carefully with Antonio, depressed by the fact that there were more columns in red than black.

"I wish," she said firmly, "to turn the Castello into a hotel."

There was a shocked silence.

Finally, he said, "My dear girl, I can only admire your courage."

The latter was said with a tone that implied she was totally, utterly, mad and naive in the extreme. She pressed on.

"And I would like to apply for an overdraft."

Without waiting for an instant rebuff, she continued, "I have gone through the costings carefully." She had had several quotes from local builders and enquired as to their reputations to make sure they were reliable and honest. "This is the quotation I am interested in, to convert parts of the bedrooms into bathrooms. I will also need extra kitchen equipment, cutlery, china, and glasses for which I have costed this," she handed over the relevant papers. "I have asked about insurance costs for fire damage and possible accidental injury or food poisoning and this is the quote for that. Then there are costs for marketing and publicity for which I have allowed this much." Another sheet of paper. She had done nearly three years of her business degree so she was not totally without an idea of what was involved.

She paused, watching his face carefully. He was inscrutable. "I will of course also have to employ extra staff as well as a manager. In total, I will need..." She named a sum.

She was holding her breath so hard she felt faint.

Of all the reactions she was expecting, his was the most unexpected.

He laughed.

But it was a laugh of admiration, not of scorn.

"Gabriella," he said. "You are amazing. I have had many clients in here asking for money but few of them have done their homework in such a thorough manner. I must be getting feeble in my old age but I am prepared to give you the money."

She almost rose to her feet and rushed to embrace him but she had to remain professional.

Then came the sting in the tail.

"Many people think they can start a hotel but it is not as easy as you think. And you do realise that if you fail, the Castello will belong to the bank?" He was now serious.

She nodded. "Well, I'd better not fail then, hadn't I?"

She rose. "Thank you very much for having faith in me. I won't let you down."

This time he shook her hand. "In Bocca al Lupo, Gabriella, in Bocca al Lupo."

And as she drove away, she mused on the old Italian blessing 'In the Mouth of the Wolf,' to wish someone good luck. It came from the twins Romulus and Remus who were abandoned as babies and who were suckled and nurtured by a she-wolf. When they grew up, they went on to found the city of Rome. She would certainly need all that luck now. She certainly didn't want a city as big as Rome, just to make a success of her own small part of Italy.

Chapter 5

She had spoken to all the staff. Antonio had of course consulted Carmela after he and Gabriella had had their first conversation. Gabriella had laughed happily at Carmela's reaction.

"Finalmente! At last." Carmela had clapped her hands in glee. "I will have the chance to show what I can do."

Gabriella had told her that she would have extra help in the kitchen and again Carmela seemed to relish the thought of having people to give orders to. She had gone away singing and Gabriella grinned at her departing back. If all the staff were like her she would have no problems.

Antonio of course would stand by her whatever she did. Tommaso as the driver, come handyman, seemed to like the idea of helping renovate some of the neglected rooms. Rosanna, her old nanny, was prepared to be a housekeeper.

They were her key positions…all except one. The manager.

A month later, she was interviewing people for the position. She had approached local agencies and seen some likely prospects. Aside from their professional qualifications she also wanted someone who she would be happy to work with, someone with whom she could get along on a personal level, be part of a team.

After a few weeks, she was beginning to doubt that she would ever find that person. Some seemed to see the job as a chance to be a kind of Lord of the Manor, even to usurp her position. Others were obviously plainly lazy or incompetent. One came to the interview looking unkempt and even had the temerity to put his feet up on the desk as he spoke to her.

She was beginning to despair that she would ever find the right person. Work had already started on converting small bedrooms and large alcoves into bathrooms and the place was ringing with the sound of hammering and sawing with workmen trailing dust everywhere. Precious china and pictures had been put away for safe keeping together with portraits of previous generations of nobility going back to the times of the Medici in Florence: counts and countesses from history who looked down haughtily from their gilded frames.

They had taken up the antique rugs and covered the precious furniture with dust sheets and the floors with plastic sheeting, but it felt like every day was a fight against dirt and chaos. Even outside, the neglected tennis court had to be resurfaced and the net renewed, the small swimming pool retiled at the edges and the steps replaced to make it completely safe.

Carmela, meanwhile, was happily occupied in her kitchen, planning menus and dreaming of Michelin stars. Rosanna was busy sourcing mattresses and duvets, pillows and cushions. They both seemed to be in their element, humming as they worked.

Another week passed; another failed interview.

Then came a huge surprise. She opened an email containing a CV from a young man living and working in London by the name of Joshua Linley.

She was intrigued. How had he come to hear of her?

She read down the first page and excitement stirred in her. He was an under manager at one of London's top hotels with experience in all departments. He had gone to Glion in Switzerland, to one of the best hotel schools in the world. Not only that, he was half-Italian and stated that his mother came from a village near Assisi. He spoke fluent Italian as well as French and German. He wished for a fresh challenge and had been advised by a friend that she was looking for a manager.

It was a complete mystery.

However, she emailed the address she had been given, stating that she would be happy to interview him over Zoom, then if he was suitable and was willing to come to Italy, then she would see him in person.

She waited eagerly for the reply.

It was even better news than she had expected. He was coming on holiday to Italy and would be staying with his aunt near Assisi the following week. Could she see him then?

She could.

She rang Flick who she realised remorsefully she had neglected horribly since her abrupt departure, only ringing briefly once to tell her of her plans. Flick was delighted to hear from her. "We've got a new flatmate," she burbled. "Not nearly as much fun as you, but at least she does her share of the washing up."

Gabriella felt an instant pang of loss for the life she had led, for those carefree student days.

"Flick?" She said, when she could at last get a word in edgeways. "Have you mentioned to anyone that I needed a manager?"

There was a squeal of excitement. "He's got in touch!"

"Who?"

"The man on the train of course."

"What!"

"You remember. That day on the tube? I gave him your number. I had his and I rang him to tell him what had happened to you. He had already tried to get in touch but of course, you had gone."

So much had happened since that fateful day that it took a moment for Gabriella to connect with what Flick was saying and then the events of that day in London came flooding back. That moment of recognition; the way she had hoped that Flick had caught the gorgeous young man before he disappeared again.

"Of course, that night I got the call about my father and I dashed to Italy leaving my English mobile behind," breathed Gabriella. "I use a different phone here. I never got the call."

"When I explained he sounded genuinely disappointed," Flick went on. "He said he would give it a while and then get in touch. I rang him and told him you weren't coming back and let him know what you were planning. Oh, this is all so exciting. Kismet, fate." She gabbled on.

"Flick!" Gabriella interrupted urgently. "Did you get his name?"

"Of course. It's Josh."

Gabriella's heart was beating wildly.

"Joshua Linley. I have his CV here on the desk in front of me. I am interviewing him for the job of manager here next week."

Another squeal from Flick. "It's definitely fate. Aren't you glad I chased after him or you might never have heard from him again?"

Gabriella laughed. "But he still has to be suitable for the job."

"Oh, he will be, of course he will be. Suitable in absolutely every possible way." Flick giggled.

Gabriella switched off her phone and her heart was pounding. She reached down to stroke Lupo and sensing her excitement, the dog laid his head on her knee as if to say 'I am with you whenever you need me.'

Chapter 6

To say that the interview was awkward at first was an understatement.

She waited for him to arrive with a mixture of excitement, curiosity and embarrassment. Lupo sat at her side and she stroked his head, as much to calm her nerves as anything.

He came through the door, a tall rangy figure in a smart suit, exuding calm and professionalism and there was a moment when time stood still for both of them.

They gazed at each other, and on Gabriella's part at least, there was that same sense of recognition that she had felt on the train that time, as if she had known this man was going to be a major part of her life. Was this how her father had felt, she wondered, when he had first set eyes on her mother?

Then she took herself firmly in hand and said to herself that whatever had brought him here it was the job that was important and she must be professional. She walked forward and shook his hand. Again there was that frisson of excitement and she held his hand a moment longer than was strictly necessary.

What was she to do? She couldn't ignore what had happened when they had seen each other before. She read in his eyes the same dilemma.

She made up her mind.

"It is good to meet you properly at last." Her tone was as light as she could make it considering the turmoil she was feeling inside. "You must forgive my friend's rather impulsive gesture. She's a dear person but rather given to mad extravagant actions. I hope she didn't embarrass you."

There was a moment's hesitation on his part before he said, "No, not at all. Shall we put all that behind us and pretend we have never seen each other before?" He was smiling, looking directly into her eyes.

She indicated a seat and sat near him, not too near and not behind a desk. It was important that she establish a proper working rapport with him, understand what made him tick and if she could work with him.

"Tell me about yourself," she said.

He told her about his past experience, repeating some of the things he had already put on his CV but which she wanted to be reassured about. He was twenty-eight. For four years, he attended University in Glion, Switzerland, one of the best in the world, covering all aspects of hotel management, including accounting, languages and culinary skills where he obtained a master's degree in international hotel business. Since then, he had worked in two top London hotels, at first in the kitchens as a kitchen porter doing the washing up and removing the rubbish, then progressing through the ranks working in every department.

"I think," he said, "that it is important that we experience every aspect of the hotel industry and know what it is like to work even at the most menial jobs. Every member of staff is part of a chain and everyone is valuable." He was now an assistant manager ready to step in when the manager was away, so he was more than qualified.

Tick number one. He was prepared to work hard and value his staff. She stressed that he would have to get on with Antonio, Carmela and the others, to be firm but fair and understand that they had lived on the estate for all their working lives and were not to be treated as mere servants. That was the first essential in her eyes.

He told her he had to give three months' notice but that he was already owed six weeks' leave so could start in a couple of months' time. They discussed his salary and agreed on a sum not quite equivalent to what he was getting in England but with the possibility of an increase when things went well.

Tick number two.

She took him round the building, Lupo following closely at her heels, showing him the work in progress. Occasionally, he frowned and suggested a few minor alterations if it wasn't too late to change things. Each time she could see he was right and was glad to have these things pointed out.

Tick number three. He had an eye for detail and made practical suggestions that would save her money.

He continued to make comments as they walked; how to make the most of each space, how to turn one of the smaller rooms downstairs into a working bar; how to overcome the problem of the distance between the kitchen and the potential dining room. In fact, there was a solution to most of the problems she had been encountering and she found herself fired up with enthusiasm. She even found herself laughing which she hadn't done much in the months following her father's death.

He told her that although he had been brought up in England, he had visited his aunt, his mother's sister, frequently for holidays in neighbouring Umbria, so he was used to Italy and Italian ways.

Tick, tick, tick.

"This is a wonderful place," he said as they stood on the terrace gazing out at the vineyards, olive groves and fields of sunflowers, "people will flock here. It is a true Tuscan idyll. I know nothing about vineyards and olive trees though…the finished product of course," he smiled, "but the process no."

"Don't worry, Antonio our estate manager deals with all that. You would only have to help me develop the house into an efficient hotel."

"Does that mean I have the job?" He said looking at her directly.

"Of course. If you want it. When can you start?"

He didn't hesitate. He smiled again. Then he said, "As soon as possible. I will let you know. But perhaps it would be a good idea if I met the owner first and make sure she approves of me."

Gabriella was confused. "Oh, I thought you understood. I am the owner."

His face changed. He looked as if he had received a severe blow. There was a very long pause

"Oh, I am so sorry. Your friend didn't tell me. I thought you worked here on behalf of the owner. Does that mean you are…" he seemed to have trouble getting the words out, "the Contessa? I was imagining some old lady dripping with jewels, not…"

"A girl who usually wears a t-shirt and jeans with a ponytail," she finished for him.

She could see he was severely thrown by the revelation.

"Does that mean you've changed your mind about the job?" She asked, trying not to betray the anxiety she felt that he would now say he had,

He went very quiet. She found herself praying desperately. 'Please, please say you'll stay' but she couldn't say it out loud. In her anxiety, she fondled Lupo's head to calm herself.

Finally, after a pause which felt like an eternity, he made up his mind. "Yes, if you want me, I will come. I felt like a fresh challenge and this will certainly be one. I've never worked in such a small hotel before or a place that started from scratch but I wanted to try working in Italy for a change. London life is interesting but very stultifying and I longed to be in the countryside again."

"Thank you," she said, feeling an over-whelming sense of relief. "Now let me introduce you to some of the people you will be working with."

But she could see that something in his attitude had changed towards her.

Changed dramatically.

Damn, damn, damn, she thought. Why should a title become such a curse? It's only a name, for heaven's sake. It had long ago failed to mean there was any power attached to it or any money for that matter. Only an enormous overdraft and the threat of losing her home if she didn't repay it.

Nevertheless, she took heart when she walked first to the estate office where they found Antonio deep in his accounts. He looked up and smiled when he saw Gabriella.

She moved forward taking Josh with her. "This is Josh Linley, Antonio, and I am very pleased to say that I have offered him the job of manager of the hotel and he has accepted."

"Piacere, pleased to meet you." The two men shook hands and she could see Antonio scrutinising Josh. She could also see because of the warmth in his voice when they talked and the fact that she knew Antonio so well that he approved of what he saw. Her instincts were right. This was the right man for the job. Antonio was a good judge of character.

They talked a little about the estate and Antonio assured Josh that he was in charge of everything outside of the main Castello building and that he didn't need to worry about that side of things.

They left and went into the kitchen where Carmela and Rosanna were having coffee together. Again, Gabriella introduced them to Josh and explained that he would be coming to take over as manager in less than two months. She could see that Carmela had a hard time resisting leaping to her feet and flinging her arms around him and Rosanna too, in her more restrained way, nodded approvingly.

After the obligatory cup of coffee and a polite refusal of lunch which Carmela pressed on him, he said his aunt and uncle were expecting him back, so he must take his leave. She looked back as they left the kitchen and Carmela lifted her hand to her cheek, making a fist with the thumb extended and softly stroking her face in that age-old gesture which means in Italian that something or someone is very special, not to mention good looking. Gabriella grinned at her.

In the office, they discussed a few more important details such as where he would live, in an attic room at the top of the Castello as she would now be doing and then all too soon he was gone. Once again, they shook hands and his touch was irresistible.

She watched his car speed away down the long drive and couldn't help but give a little silent prayer of thanks that he would be coming to share some of the problems, mingled with certainty that her first instincts on that day on the tube in London had been the right ones.

She was sure, very sure that he was the man on whom her future depended.

In more ways than one.

Chapter 7

The next few weeks flew by in a whirl of activity. Every day brought fresh problems. Plumbing problems, supply problems, problems with endless form filling. She hadn't bargained on the number of permits she had to have before she was allowed to open as a hotel. Insurance for any number of things, fire, flood, food poisoning and theft, alcohol licences, food regulations, insurance for Tommaso and herself to drive the guests, employment regulations and telephone lines. It took hours to fill in each one, checking and rechecking for possibly expensive mistakes. They were inspected by planners, fire chiefs and hygiene inspectors: every other day, it seemed, another person with a clip board appeared at the front door.

Then there was the problem of the laundry. To send it out, which would be expensive, or build a facility in the basement? She waited for workmen who didn't turn up and others, because she was a woman she suspected, thought she wouldn't be able to tell if they'd done a good job or not. And again, because everyone was new at the hotel game, they all demanded her attention. She would be in the middle of an important phone call and Carmela would come from the kitchen to ask how many pans she was allowed to order, or Tommaso came to say he had run out of nails and cement and could he go off and buy some? She tried to keep her temper and not snap at them. After all, she was the one in charge and it was better they ask her rather than make a mistake. She fell into bed each night, exhausted, and then would wake in the small hours, worrying, thoughts and problems crowding her brain. On other nights, her pillow would be wet with tears, remembering her father but also resenting him because he had left her with this overwhelming, impossible task of saving the Castello.

She raged into her pillow trying to muffle her sobs so the rest of the household couldn't hear her, comforted only by the constant presence of Lupo in his bed in the corner of the room who came to nuzzle her frequently as she wept, seeking as much comfort from her as she did from him, as she knew he had been a one-man dog who had lost his master and was as bereft as she was.

But then, she reminded herself sternly, it had been her choice; hers alone. She could have given in to the inevitable, tried to struggle on, then maybe have to sell the Castello in the end and return to London to finish her studies and make a new independent life for herself. Her title would open a few doors for her but that would only take her so far. It had been her choice to turn the Castello into a hotel and she was not going to fail.

She was not, she told herself sternly.

So every morning she got up, took a shower, pulled on her jeans and a fresh t-shirt and went to face the day and whatever problems it would throw at her.

She did take time every day though to visit her father's grave, Lupo with her, both of them lying on the grass near his favourite place where they had buried him on a sunny slope facing the foothills of the mountains and next to his beloved wife with whom he had always talked of being united one day. She told him of her plans and how she missed him and hoped he would have been proud of her and was sorry she was angry with him for leaving her like that. There was no family to lean on either, to come to her aid. The count had been the last of his generation apart from a few elderly great aunts and uncles and her mother had been an only child with her parents both long gone.

However, she longed for the day that Josh would arrive and take over. She could only hope that he was all she expected him to be. She worried that she was replacing a dead father with someone else to rely on, fantasising that he could support her emotionally as well as in the great task of getting the hotel up and running. He might not be in the end the person she had thought him to be. It might just have been a romantic fantasy, a moment of student wishful thinking.

She firmly pushed such negative thoughts out of her mind and turned to the matters in hand, of which there were many.

Josh had left her with several mantras, one of which was to buy the best she could. "If you buy cheap fittings they will only have to be replaced in a year or so."

Cutlery and china had to be bought and the valuable pieces inherited through generations, some of them dating from Renaissance times, would be for display only. They were part of the history of the house it was true, but life was moving on and they had to adapt to this new way of living and some antiques, especially those dating back centuries, could fetch a considerable sum if they were sold. It was certainly something to consider, especially as, with strangers in the place, which is what most of the hotel guests would be, everything would have to be insured.

Then there was linen to be purchased, both for the table and beds. The embroidered bedlinen edged with handmade lace which had come as part of her mother's and even her grandmother's trousseaux had never been very practical and was even less so now, needing as they did, hours of ironing.

Rosanna, now her housekeeper, was relishing the fact that she was needed again. She had done her homework and helped Gabriella choose more practical bedding. They sat together, the older woman as thin and wrinkled as Carmela was round and shiny like an apple, Rosanna marvelling at the decisive and competent woman she had helped to raise.

Rosanna had been the one to tuck her up in bed most nights when she was little, reading her bedtime stories, kissing her goodnight with the words 'Sogni d'Oro', 'dreams of gold', that traditional charming Italian blessing

It had been Rosanna who had bought her new clothes as she grew, although her old-fashioned ideas had sometimes caused friction between the pair of them, especially when Gabriella was a teenager and given to door slamming and uttering the immortal phrase of teenagers everywhere 'I hate you, I hate you' whereupon Rosanna would sigh and wait patiently for the moment when, inevitably, a tear-stained Gabriella would come back into the room and say, "Sorry, I didn't really mean it," and Rosanna would cuddle her and soothe her…until the next battle.

From the first, though, her curiosity about her dead mother had always been at the forefront of her mind. She knew from experience that asking her father was no use. He would just say, "She was wonderful in every way," and then his face would crumple and he would start to cry. So it was to Rosanna she turned to ask her questions.

"Tell me what my mother was like," she used to command in her childish voice from the first moment she realised that she had had a mother at all.

"Well, she was very pretty, just like you," Rosanna would answer, "and sometimes very naughty, just like you." And Gabriella would giggle.

Then as she grew older and said, "What was my mother really like?"

Rosanna would reply, "Go and look in the mirror. You are just like her, almost identical in every way."

"Oh," Gabriella would reply, "Is that why Papa looks at me sometimes and I see tears come into his eyes because I remind him of her?"

"Maybe it is," Rosanna would answer, "but in a good way of course."

Then she would add, "You are like her in character as well. She was very strong-willed. I think if she wanted something very badly your father didn't stand a chance. He knew when it was easier just to say yes and not have a battle on his hands." She would smile at the memory.

"Is that bad?"

"Not if you use it in the right way. If you are determined to succeed and you persevere, you will never give up until you get what you want."

Then when she was even older she asked, "Does Papa blame me for my mother's death?"

Rosanna had looked at her in astonishment. "Of course not. A baby can't be blamed for a childbirth that went wrong. It happened in those days, many women died because medicine was not as good as it is now."

Gabriella never stopped asking questions. "Where did my mother come from?" was one such.

"She was the daughter of one of the estate workers but there are no members of the family left there now."

"Oh, she wasn't a countess then, I mean before she married Papa?"

"Far from it. There was great opposition from your grandfather, of course, because she wasn't of so-called noble birth, but your father was determined and your grandfather had to give in in the end. I was only a young girl, long before I came to look after you. I worked here as a housemaid and I would hear the loud arguments coming from behind the study door, we all could, with your father first begging and pleading, your grandfather telling him he was dragging a noble family into the dirt, that he had to marry someone of noble line, preferably with money to spare to keep up the repairs on the Castello; your father insisting that he loved your mother and that he would never marry anyone purely for money. Your grandfather insisted that she only wanted to marry him to become a countess and not because she loved him; your father equally insisted that he knew it was true love on both sides and that she was the only person to make him happy and what kind of father didn't care about his son's happiness? The rows went on for months but your father stuck to his guns."

"Good for Papa."

"Yes, in the end, your father prevailed. They were meeting in secret all the time, down in the olive groves. The wedding took place but it was a small affair with no grand guests because your grandfather said he wasn't going to waste money on an affair that would end badly, but I've been to many weddings in my time and that was the happiest I've ever seen. The pair of them absolutely radiated love. They only had eyes for each other. They had three years together, hardly out of each other's sight. Then she was pregnant with you and the night she went into labour, there was a terrible storm and it was a difficult birth and although they called the doctor he didn't arrive in time. I have never seen such despair as that on your father's face. He howled like a dog and he wouldn't let her be taken away for two days. He shut himself in his room then and no one could reach him. Eventually, it was Antonio who persuaded him to come out."

"Poor Papa," Gabriella whispered.

"But it was you that saved him. A wet nurse was hired to feed you but otherwise, he wouldn't let you out of his sight. He hung over your cot day and night and gradually his delight in watching you grow and looking after you saved him from his depression."

"I'm glad. I hope he was proud of me, that I never let him down."

"Oh never, not once," Rosanna replied. "No father could have been prouder of a daughter. You always studied hard at school and were always top of your class and when you went to London to study, he missed you so much."

That latter conversation had only happened recently.

"At least I think he knew I was here at the end and I hope my parents are united somewhere in heaven. I also hope I can find someone I love as much as that and that it has a happier ending."

"I am sure you will find someone who deserves you. You are very special and they have to be very special too."

Now, as they sat together talking of more mundane things like bedlinen, Gabriella was reminded of those talks they had had and, on an impulse, she leaned over and kissed Rosanna on the cheek.

Rosanna looked up in astonishment. "What was that for?"

"Just for being there for me when I was growing up and looking after me so well."

Rosanna gazed back at her and smiled. "It has been the greatest privilege of my life, seeing you grow up to be the wonderful woman you have become," she said simply.

Rosanna wasn't her only mother figure though and Gabriella realised that she was incredibly lucky to have two such women in her life. While Rosanna held sway upstairs, her life with Carmela was in the kitchen where she was fed every day until she was old enough to sit with her father and his guests at the dinner table.

Having never known any other way, Gabriella considered both these women as her family and adored them both. There was no rivalry between them for her affection as their sole aim in life was to make Gabriella feel happy and safe and in that, they had succeeded admirably.

So now while Rosanna and Gabriella were choosing bed linen, Carmela was making lists of things she would need in the kitchen, in her element, round cheeks gleaming. She looked ten years younger, excited and confident as she bossed her new assistant Lucia around.

Carmela and Gabriella between them had interviewed quite a few girls who professed to be able to cook but Carmela had been surprisingly strict, asking them all manner of questions about herbs, spices and traditional recipes. She had then asked them to make a cake and had sat watching with an eagle eye as they mixed the ingredients. Several of the candidates had gone away in tears, unable to complete the task to Carmela's exacting standards, but Lucia had passed with flying colours. She had come from a trattoria in the city and was a cheerful, smiling, competent girl who was a mini Carmela in all respects and didn't seem to mind Carmela instructing her in every detail, bossing her round, making sure she scrubbed every pan religiously and polished the copper to Carmela's exacting standards, which luckily she did.

The sight made Gabriella smile as she came downstairs.

She had taken on a local boy and girl, Marco a young man with a winning smile who Gabriella knew would be a hit with the guests and Gianetta, quieter but obviously efficient. They both spoke several languages, had worked in hotels abroad and were employed to help in the bedrooms, dining room and bar, wherever they were needed most. She wanted Josh to train them to be proficient in all areas. In a small hotel, he had told her, everyone had to multitask. There was no room for hierarchy. You couldn't expect staff to do the menial, even unpleasant things, she reasoned, if you yourself weren't prepared to do them yourself.

Tommaso was kept busy taking deliveries, helping with decorating and general handiwork and she heard him whistling as he worked, which she took to be a good sign. There was a general air of optimism and purpose around and she took strength and hope from that.

Josh was constantly in touch from England, keeping conversations professional and to the point, but she found herself jumping eagerly every time the phone rang. She longed for support as far as the hotel was concerned and any thoughts about the spark that existed between them had to be firmly suppressed. Both Carmela and Antonio were keeping an eye on her, soothing her when she got stressed, as she often did when deliveries didn't arrive, contractors didn't turn up and when, heaven forfend, a leak developed in one of the new bathrooms.

She longed for the day though when she could share the burden.

Chapter 8

At the sight of his tall, rangy figure getting out of the taxi that had brought him from Florence airport, she had to restrain herself from rushing out and flinging her arms around him. She gathered herself together and went out to meet him. "I'm so glad you are here," she said simply.

"I'm glad too," he smiled. "I am relishing the challenge. Let me get settled then you can show me what you have been doing."

She showed him upstairs to his attic room and asked anxiously if he would be alright. "You will have to share a bathroom I'm afraid. The best rooms we have to reserve for the guests of course. I myself have moved up here at the far end of the landing."

"It will be fine," he smiled. "I've lived in a lot worse, believe you me."

She left him to get settled and then showed him the progress that had been made since his last visit. The twelve bedrooms were beautiful, all of them large and spacious with frescoed ceilings, some with four-poster beds, all with huge windows with marvellous views of the hills, the fields and the olive groves. They stood together looking out and she said, "Leonardo da Vinci is supposed to have painted here. The background to The Mona Lisa is very like that view over there," she pointed. "This area is counted as the birthplace of the Renaissance where Michelangelo and Galileo worked."

"Fabulous," he said. "We need to get working on the publicity as soon as possible. Tell me more about the history of the place." She told him the story of her family, how her father, the count, had inherited the land from his father and then way back to Renaissance times and the Medici family. They came under the jurisdiction of Arezzo, a walled city state once as important in its time as Florence or Siena when, in medieval times, the city states had been at war with one another. Tuscany in fact could boast seven World Heritage sites, including Florence, Pisa, Pienza, Siena, San Gimignano, the Val d'Orcia, a rich verdant valley in southern Tuscany where the River Orcia ran, and the Medici gardens and villas. "Yes," he said matter of factly, "we must also stress the fact that you are a countess. People love a royal connection." There was no trace of the awkwardness, that moment when he had gone quiet as he first discovered the fact of her title. She could see he was the consummate professional, able to divide his working life from any private feelings he might have. "We need to get in touch with all the tourist offices, then spread out worldwide. I have contacts in London."

"And I have contacts locally," Gabriella interrupted eagerly. "I have already been in touch with a few of them."

"Good, good. We need to get brochures printed, set up a website, organise some dates for journalists to come and write us up."

"Yes, yes and I must take you to see our bank manager. I am sure he will want to see that I have a professional in charge rather than just a headstrong girl who doesn't realise quite what she has taken on." She grinned and was relieved to see that he smiled back.

. . . .

With Josh at the helm, Gabriella felt she could spare an hour to take her mare, Tosca, out for an hour's ride in the hills. She swung thankfully into the saddle and urged the horse into a canter, relishing the feeling of the wind in her face, the sense of freedom. Oh how she had missed this in London, especially when it was winter, the days were dark and dreary and the city was crowded and noisy: then she had longed for the countryside of home. This is where she belonged; it was in her blood, in her veins. Lupo ran behind the horse, keeping up every step of the way as they galloped through the estate and out towards the distant hills.

Tosca had been a present from her father for her eighteenth birthday. She remembered only too well that moment when he said he had a special surprise for her and made her cover her eyes as he led her outside. They had always had horses, as the count himself had been a more than accomplished horseman, but she herself had started riding at the age of two on a small pony, graduating every few years to larger horses, but she had never had one as swift and agile as Tosca. She had uncovered her eyes and gasped at the sight of the beautiful chestnut mare with the flowing black mane. She had moved forward in wonderment, tears of joy springing into her eyes, being careful not to startle the horse. She had stroked her neck, marvelling at her rich colour and the smooth texture of her skin, with the powerful rippling muscles which showed her breeding.

Now she galloped on until finally, reluctantly, she returned to the stable and slipped off the horse.

Josh was waiting for her as she led Tosca into her stall. She removed the horse's saddle and brushed her down.

"I've arranged for some local journalists to come for a drink early next month if that's alright. I think we will have enough to show them by then," he said.

"Excellent," she said. "What about foreign journalists, travel writers?"

"They are more complicated," Josh replied. "They'll have to stay of course, so we'll have to be almost completely ready before they come, but I'm putting out feelers." He smiled and involuntarily reached out a hand to brush a strand of hair from her forehead that threatened to cover her eye. She held her breath. "Sorry," he muttered, for a moment losing his professional cool. There was an awkward pause. She moved towards him, her lips parted. His eyes held hers. This was the moment she had long been anticipating.

"Gabriella," It was Antonio coming towards them. "Carmela needs you in the kitchen. Something about the range misfiring."

"I'll come at once. Thank you, Antonio. Excuse me, Josh." She hurried off, her cheeks burning.

Chapter 9

She lay awake that night tossing restlessly, wondering if he was doing the same. Surely, she thought he wouldn't have given up his big job in London on a whim if he hadn't felt the same attraction that she felt. Or was it just a coincidence that he saw it as a good opportunity to be back in Italy where his mother came from? His reaction when he discovered her title meant surely that he had previously had hopes of getting to know her better. But then he had seemed put off by that exact discovery.

Oh, it was all such a muddle.

She finally fell into an exhausted sleep around dawn. She was glad the next day for a chance to escape, to drive herself the fifteen kilometres into Arezzo to visit the tourist office and the printers. She left the autostrada, driving towards the city on the floodplain of the river Arno. On the city's highest point, she could see the spire of the Duomo, the elegant sandstone cathedral, majestically dominating the medieval centre, a cathedral where the great and good of the city had been buried including Pope Gregory X.

And of course, only too recently, it had been the scene of her father's funeral mass, but she tried not to dwell on that fact. She parked at the foot of the hill and used the convenient escalator from the lower road to take her up to the oldest part of the city, the Centro Storico, the historic centre, which remained much as it was in medieval times and even further back to Etruscan and Roman times, with its narrow cobbled streets and alleyways, tiny hidden squares and courtyards. The city had spread out into the valley below over the years and citizens who lived outside the walls had been relieved when the escalator had been built, saving them the long climb on foot to the centre with its many shops, restaurants and flourishing cafes. It was a city close to her heart. It was always spotlessly clean, the rubbish collected by the little three-wheel buzzing Ape trucks every day, aptly named after bees, as that is what they sounded like. The streets too were swept every morning and it was a place where you could wander late at night and feel safe with no drunks to disturb the peace. The tourist office was next to the cathedral and opposite it was the ancient town hall, the Commune, flags flying from the top and looking very like a castle.

She chatted a while with the pleasant girl in charge who was very interested in her plans and said she was looking forward to coming to see the Castello just before they opened so she could recommend the facilities to visiting tourists. Gabriella then got quotes from two different printers for publicity leaflets and brochures for the hotel, discussing layouts and various qualities of paper and so on. By the time she had finished, she was hungry and thirsty. She walked back up the Corso, the main shopping street from the printers towards the Piazza Grande, the central square of the city. On the way, she popped into one of the stores. She had decided that she needed to smarten up her wardrobe. She had never needed formal clothes before, having worn t-shirts, jeans and baggy jumpers as a student, with the odd evening dress for special occasions. She had looked through the clothes she had left at home and many of them were outdated, some even things she had worn as a child. It was a nostalgic process as many of the outfits she pulled out reminded her of happy times with her father or with her grandparents, all sadly long since passed away. She had resolutely bundled many of them up and dropped them off at a charity shop on the way into the city. Now it was time to buy a couple of jackets, smart blouses, skirts and a trouser suit for her new career.

So, laden down with carrier bags she at last entered the square, glancing up at the main entrance of the Pieve, the thirteenth-century abbey, as she passed. It was one of her favourite spots in the city with its relief carvings of figures at work in the fields depicting all four of the seasons on the arched doorway. She entered the loggia, the covered walkway, dominating the top of the square, designed by the artist and architect Giorgio Vasari, a son of Arezzo and the biographer of all the Renaissance artists. She found a table in the shade, ordered a spremuta, a cold drink of fresh lemon juice, and a panino of prosciutto. She sat gazing down the sloping square at the tall ancient palazzos with their terracotta roofs, the curved rear of the abbey with its serried rows of columns, one of which was twisted the wrong way, probably, she had always thought, to remind people that only God was perfect. Then there was the fountain where pigeons were busily preening themselves in the rushing water and the old well on the opposite side. Above her, she heard music issuing from the open windows of the music school over the loggia. Alongside her, the clock on the old courthouse, the

Tribunale chimed one o'clock. She thought for the first time that this was one of the most beautiful squares in Italy and yet it was much less well-known than its more famous cousins in Florence and Siena.

One of the things she intended to do was take guests on guided tours, both here and to some of the many beautiful and historic villages of Tuscany. She glanced up to where an elderly woman was watering her little rooftop garden and a cat walked across the tiles before lying down to the sun itself in the most convenient spot. She smiled. So many memories from her childhood: a tear came into her eye as she thought about her father carrying her on his shoulders through the square when she was a small girl and how she had felt a mile tall. Even more memories of her father came into her mind as she glanced up at the palazzo, the tall building to her left, which belonged to the Castello estate. She had no time to visit it now but she remembered all the times she and her father had sat together on the extensive balcony watching various spectacles in the square, the twice-yearly Joust of the Saracen, the open-air concerts on the steps of the Tribunale, the monthly antique markets with their crowded trestle tables crammed with goods and the sparkling lights of the Christmas market which had so excited her as a small girl. It would be a very useful stop-off point for future guests when they come into the city. She smiled to herself as she thought of the day when her father had forgotten to switch off the fine electric wire that ran along the top of the balustrade to deter the pigeons and had given himself an electric shock…fortunately only a very mild one but it had become their custom to shout 'switch off the pigeon wire' ever afterwards as soon as they entered.

Sometimes though she and her father had just sat there in companionable silence admiring the comings and goings of the citizens; the cat that followed an elderly man on his early morning walk as if it were a dog, the children on their way to school, the tourists standing in admiration as they gazed around them, the swifts screaming round in the evening air in search of insects, the brilliant sunsets on the mountains that they could glimpse through the gap to the left of the Pieve and even the sight of the square covered in snow as they watched in amusement or concern as people slipped and slid on the icy surface. Oh, how she missed her father. She felt a surge of emotion and her feelings threatened to overwhelm her at that moment. "Papa," she whispered to herself, "I will make you proud of me, I promise I will." Then gathering herself together, she rose to make her way back to her waiting car.

Wandering along, her mind full of memories, she did not notice at first the couple coming towards her until she nearly bumped into them.

"Buongiorno, Gabriella," the voice came from somewhere in front of her.

She stopped, startled out of her reverie.

It was her cousin Domenico and his mother.

She knew that Domenico had told everyone that would listen that it was he who should have inherited the Castello on the death of the count, not a mere girl, but had been firmly reminded by the solicitor after the reading of the Will that the days when only a male relative could inherit were long since gone and try as he might to overturn the count's wishes there was no way he could contest it. She was aware though that the resentment simmered on.

It took a strong resolve to smile at them and be civil. They were both as oily and insincere as ever and she remembered their copious crocodile tears at the funeral. She could see Domenico's rictus smile on his skeletal face, his yellowed teeth and stringy, greasy hair, obviously dyed jet black in an attempt to look younger. His mother was much the same, but her face, over-powdered and with bright lipstick slightly smeared at the edges looked more like some sort of caricature instead of the beauty she imagined herself to be. Her hair, which Gabriella remembered as blonde, was dyed a brassy shade of yellow and stiffened with vast quantities of hair lacquer into a rigid helmet in a vain attempt to disguise the fact that it was thinning. Domenico grimaced at her now in what passed as a smile, embracing her in his bony arms. She tried not to shudder as he pecked formally at both her cheeks. His mother did the same.

"My dear, Gabriella. How are you? You poor thing! What troubles you must be having. We have heard that you are having to descend to opening your home to the public. How dreadful that must be and how sad that your father, God rest his soul, left you in such desperate circumstances."

Gabriella took a deep breath. "Well," she said, "it's actually quite exciting. I think the days when landed people kept huge estates to themselves are over, don't you? It's time to share them and go into business, explore a new direction."

"Ah," Cara said, "you always were a bit of a rebel, a little left-wing…even a…socialist," she stressed the last word with a shudder as if she had uttered a forbidden word, smiling her awful smile and reminding Gabriella so much of Cruella de Ville that despite herself, she almost giggled. "Alas, the old days are gone I fear," Cara continued, "when one had control of one's servants. They all want to be our equal nowadays."

"If you mean by servants, I have loyal staff and I owe everything to them. They have stood by me and supported me wholeheartedly through these last months, indeed throughout my whole life: and several of them, Antonio in particular, my father counted as a dear friend and confidante." She tried hard to keep her temper.

"But of course, my dear, you think that if you must. And we will come and support you when you open and we will bring our friends."

"That will be lovely," replied Gabriella, "just ring when you are ready and make a booking."

"And of course, dear Gabriella, I am sure Domenico is always ready to give you good advice when you need it. You only have to ask." Gabriella bit her lip so hard she thought she might have drawn blood. She refrained from retorting that Domenico was the last person on earth she would go to for advice.

"If you will excuse me," she said, "I really must get back. Duty calls."

"But of course." Domenico made a great show of seizing her hand, raising it to his lips and kissing it extravagantly. "We will be in touch." Gabriella sped away. On an impulse, she decided not to go straight back to the car. What she really wanted to do was wash that hand thoroughly, she felt so contaminated, so revolted, by the pair of them. To calm herself, she veered right, down to the smaller square of San Francesco with its church of the same name. She entered the dim and peaceful place and walked towards the altar surrounded by wonderful frescoes of the Legend of the True Cross by the Renaissance master Piero Della Francesca, depicting the queen of Sheba visiting king Solomon. It had been a real labour of love, taking him ten years to paint them. Those serene and beautiful faces never failed to soothe her. She stood for a few moments gazing at them, and then, before leaving, lit a candle in memory of both her parents. She walked back up the hill past the Duomo again, descended the escalator, climbed into her car and drove home.

Chapter 10

Two days later, she made an appointment with Giovanni Battista the bank manager and drove back to Arezzo with Josh.

"It will be good to meet him properly," Josh had said when she suggested it. "Phone calls aren't quite the same."

Soon they were bowling down the long drive of the Castello, Gabriella speeding at her usual fast pace. Josh winced as she took the last bend into the road with a squeal of brakes, but he didn't say anything.

She glanced over at him, laughing. "Does my driving worry you? Sorry. I suppose I'm so used to this road that I don't even think about it. My father was always telling me off because I drove too fast."

She decreased her speed a little and Josh said, "What was he like, your father? I mean, don't talk about him if it upsets you. I know Antonio worshipped him, Carmela, Tommaso and Rosanna too, and I haven't heard a bad word said about him from any of the workers on the estate. He must have been quite a man."

Gabriella smiled. "He was the best, but I would say that wouldn't I? I know he was highly respected by everyone. Not many people look after their estates so well or care so much for those who work for them. He was also a champion rider, fearless in the extreme. He won the Golden Lance five times," she said proudly.

"What's the Golden Lance?" Josh asked

"Ah, you have a treat in store. The Joust of the Saracen is held twice a year. We'll be taking guests to it. Each of the four quarters of the city has two riders who have to hit a target held on the arm of a bust of a Saracen, not so easy at full gallop with a long lance on your arm."

"I look forward to it. It sounds spectacular," he said.

"It is, and of course, there is all the pageantry that goes with it, everyone in costume, the bands, the procession, the flag displays."

She was acutely aware of his thigh nearly touching hers as he sat in the passenger seat and wondered if he was aware of it too. She reached over to change gear and her hand brushed his.

'Concentrate, Gabriella. Concentrate,' she told herself sternly and tried to keep her eyes on the road ahead. They rounded the last bend and the walls of the city and the spire of the cathedral lay ahead at the very top of the Centro Storico.

Josh broke the silence, "I really don't know Arezzo at all. I spent all my holidays near Assisi, though I visited Florence a couple of times. I mean I know it's an old city."

"Very much so. A lot of it is Etruscan," Gabriella replied. "The Romans called it Aretium and it was once as important as Florence. The old fortress above the cathedral, the Duomo, was built by Cosimo I, the ruler of Florence, the most powerful of the Medicis." She paused. "When we've finished at the bank, I'll show you around."

"That would be great. Whoa," he exclaimed as she slammed on her brakes and reversed abruptly into an impossibly small gap. "That was impressive. You really are a very good driver."

She laughed. "Necessary here with so many cars and such narrow streets. You have to take your chances where you can. If you didn't know how to reverse park you would be lost. There's a car park at the bottom of the escalator on the other side but this is nearer. The bank is just up there so we can walk."

They were near the station and as they crossed the road, he asked, "What's that?"

She followed his gaze to the statue on the grassy verge of a strange-looking animal.

"Ah, the Chimera. The symbol of Arezzo. The original is in the museum in Florence. That's a copy. It's a fire -breathing female monster with a lion's head, a goat's body and a serpent's tail."

"Wow, I wouldn't like to meet one of those on a dark night. Doesn't the word also mean an illusion, an unrealistic dream?"

"Yes, I suppose it does." She felt a strange jolt as if her idea of turning the Castello into a hotel would all be an unrealistic dream after all, but she firmly dismissed the idea. Now was not a time to have doubts.

They were entering a maze of cobbled streets in the old city and she could see him looking about him as they walked along admiringly. They went into the bank together and many of the staff rose to their feet at the sight of Gabriella.

One scurried forward and took her hand, bowing over it. "Contessa, it is a privilege. Signor Battista is waiting for you in his office."

Damn, Gabriella thought, *I wish they wouldn't make such a fuss.* But it was too late. She could see Josh noting the respectful half-bows as they walked towards the back office, reminding him of her so-called status in the world.

Giovanni Battista rose to his feet as they entered. At least he treated her like any other customer, Gabriella thought with relief. He had known the family too long. She introduced Josh and they were offered chairs.

After the necessary chit-chat about health, they got down to business and Gabriella was enormously impressed by the amount of knowledge Josh had picked up already on the affairs of the estate and the Castello itself. She let him lead the conversation, only chiming in occasionally when they referred to her about some previous fact.

The interview over at last they all rose to their feet.

"Well, Gabriella," Giovanni Battista said as they made their farewells, "I can see you have a very competent young man here. I don't think we need to worry about the success of your hotel with him in charge."

Gabriella could see a flush spread across Josh's face at the praise.

"I am glad you think so. I think so too," she said simply and smiled at him.

They went back through the outer office where once again the staff bowed and murmured, 'Contessa,' as they passed. Then finally they were outside again and walking up the narrow ancient streets admiring the enormous wooden doors of the houses, some of them with huge iron studs and knockers. Some of the tops of the houses had decorative friezes and tiles and there was the sound of birdsong from little gardens hidden behind the tall walls; bright bougainvillea hung down from corners and long swathes of ivy.

They entered the square, the Piazza Grande, and he gasped, "But this is wonderful. I had no idea."

"Few people do," Gabriella answered. "They flock to Florence and Sienna but this is just as spectacular in its own way."

He gazed at the ancient abbey, the Pieve, the Tribunale with its spectacular bell tower which chose at that moment to chime the hour, at the impressive loggia at the top and the tall palazzos and towers everywhere. "This is where the joust is held," she said.

"So we can get tickets and bring the guests."

"We won't need tickets. We own the house there, the one with the balcony."
She pointed to her right, acutely aware that this was yet another example of her
status and so-called wealth. "We can serve lunch up there after a tour of all the
various rituals that are part of the ceremonies."

"Exactly," he was being the consummate professional yet again she could
see, keeping any private thoughts well hidden. "Sounds like a very good package
we'll be able to provide."

"And there's a street party the night before as well in each quarter of the city
which is great fun."

"Even better."

They stood for a moment gazing around them and watching the swifts
whirling in the air, listening to the music coming from the music school over the
loggia.

"Listen, I'm starving," she said finally, "shall we buy some panini and then
go on up to the fort? We deserve a break." They laughed together about the
English habit of calling one panino 'a panini' which of course meant more than
one.

"Great idea." So they bought two panini from one of the many cafes and a
bottle of water and she led him out of the top left-hand quarter of the square
which was the quickest way to get to the top of the city. Unfortunately, it also
passed the wall of the ancient library, the Palazzo Pretorio, its outer face
decorated with the crests of all the noble families of the area, including hers,
which of course he immediately noticed. She saw him looking but he didn't
comment.

They went up past the house of the poet Petrarch and were immediately in
sight of the Duomo.

"I'd show you around inside but…" her voice tailed off.

"Of course," he was immediately sympathetic. "Your father. I understand. It
must be still very fresh in your mind."

They turned right and went through the park lined with pine trees with its
vast statue of Petrarch ,then came to the entrance of the fort.

Passing through the sloping tunnel they climbed upwards and emerged into
the sunlight.

The views from the top were amazing. They walked round gazing at the
rooftops of the city and miles of surrounding countryside.

"What's that tower that looks like a castle?" He asked.

"It's the town hall."

"I shouldn't be surprised." He laughed. "Only in Italy can a town hall look like a castle."

They carried on, looking down at remains of excavations of Etruscan sites even older than the fort. Then views of the more modern developments spreading out below the historic centre. Finally, though there was the breathtaking view of the wooded slopes of the Apennines and it was here they found a bench and sat to eat their panini, revelling in the sunshine.

"Tell me about your parents," she said. "How did they meet?"

"My mother went as an au pair to learn English, met my father and stayed."

"It must have been fun having parents of two different nationalities."

"It was. Luckily, I was brought up to be bilingual. My mother spoke to me in Italian, my father in English, and they made sure I stayed every year with my aunt Paola, my mother's sister, so I could hear Italian spoken every day."

"Your mother must miss Italy though."

"She does, less so now though. I think at first she had to restrain herself from kissing everyone in the Italian way, though it's taken off more in England now that the English are more relaxed than they used to be. She used to complain too that everything was so quiet. She missed the noise and bustle of Italian life. She also found it hard at first to make friends, but now she has many friends and because she teaches Italian, she can convey her enthusiasm for this country too and people go to her for advice on what to see when they book an Italian holiday. And they both come over frequently of course."

"I hope to be allowed to meet them some day."

"I'm sure you will…and my Aunt Paola and Uncle Renato. They are lovely people. My aunt is a great character too. I think you would get on with her very well. You and she are very alike I think."

Gabriella blushed as she sensed that was a great compliment.

"How about you? How did you get on being the son of people from two different countries?"

He laughed again. "I think some people thought I was rather exotic. Then there are always those awful people who think only in cliches about the Italians and talk in silly accents as if we're all peasants, but I always remind them we are among the most highly educated and sophisticated societies in the world and we do have doctors and teachers and lawyers too. And then, of course, the wretched Mafia. One boy at school used to hum the Godfather theme every time I went near him and called me Don Corleone all the time. I got fed up with jokes about horse's heads on my pillow and being made an offer I couldn't refuse. Everybody thinks they are being so witty and that they are the only people who have said it. You have to remind them occasionally that we had some of the best artists in the world, some of the most beautiful cities in the world."

"Exactly." Gabriella laughed. "Then again I know people in Italy make jokes about the English and their 'stiff upper lips', the dreadful weather, awful coffee and lousy food...except I know English food has improved enormously in the last thirty years from the boiled cabbage era. The Italians used to call English coffee Aqua Sporca, dirty water, but that's improved too. I met a man in England who had been on holiday to Italy for five days and thought he knew it all. He kept saying 'hasta la vista' every time we met even though I told him that was Spanish and when I told him I came from Tuscany, he raved about the lovely pannacotta roofs. I thought at first he was joking but then I realised he wasn't and I had to explain that pannacotta was literally 'cooked cream' and the roofs were made of terracotta, literally baked earth. His final parting shot was to call me a beautiful sederino."

"What!" Josh exclaimed.

"Exactly. I almost hit him until I realised that what he had meant to say was 'signorina' and I explained that sederino was the word for bottom. He did have the grace to look embarrassed and apologised."

They giggled together and it was a moment of pure intimacy and togetherness. They looked at each other.

She thought with a jolt. *I really could fall in love with this man.*

She took a deep breath to collect herself.

"Then again," she went on after a pause, "I probably said some terrible things in English when I first arrived and people were too polite to correct me."

"Quite," he smiled, "and the same with me in Italian."

"So where do you most feel at home?"

"Both countries," he replied. "England was my home and Italy was for holidays. It's interesting that now Italy is home and it will be England for the holidays. Having two countries is wonderful I think, gives you a wider perspective and enriches your life. And," he grinned, "I wave my arms about more in Italy than I do in England of course."

"I've noticed."

"Yes, I think living in England for nearly three years made me see what was wonderful about both countries, though I don't think London life was for me long term. I longed for the countryside of Tuscany."

"And where did you go to school?" He asked.

"Oh, the local primary school. Then my father thought I should go to a convent but I only lasted a term. I hated it. The nuns were so strict and I suppose I was a bit of a rebel. Then I came here to Arezzo and went to the local secondary school which I mostly loved."

"Mostly?"

"You talk about cliches…the Mafia and so on. I was teased by some kids because of my background. They thought I was posh and took the Mickey, bowing and scraping and calling me, 'Your Majesty' every time I came near them."

He went quiet. She had reminded him yet again of her position in society.

Idiot, she thought to herself. Then she added, "I found the only way to deal with it was to go along with it and pretend to treat them as my loyal subjects. When they saw I didn't get riled or upset but acted as if it was a big joke, they soon came around. Actually one of them is one of my best friends now."

" Clever," he said. "Perhaps I should have left a few horses' heads on my tormentors' pillows."

They both grinned.

They were still smiling at each other when he went to reach out to brush a crumb from her sleeve. Then, remembering himself, he stopped abruptly.

There was an awkward silence. Then Gabriella said, "Ah well, time to go. There's work to do."

"Yes," he said. "Plenty of work if we're to be ready in time."

They went slowly back down the tunnel again, into the park and on down the hill. On the way down, they passed the front door of the Pieve.

"Oh," Josh said, "what's that up there?" He pointed to the relief sculptures of the figures decorating the porch.

"Ah, those are the Four Seasons. Lovely, aren't they? One of my favourite sights in Arezzo, thinking how they reflect the countryside and the workers."

"They're beautiful. I think that maybe it might be one of my favourite sights too. Everything is so grand and impressive but somehow," he mused, "somehow, they are something very personal."

At that moment, she felt so emotionally bonded to him, as if they felt the same way, thought the same thoughts and understood each other perfectly.

She sensed that under normal circumstances, he would now have taken her hand. They would have been like any other boyfriend and girlfriend, but there was a shadow between them and she didn't know how she was ever going to get rid of it. Was it going to be an insuperable barrier forever?

For a while, it had all been so perfect, Gabriella thought. So very peaceful in that lovely place up on the hill as if they were floating above the city and she had felt more relaxed and happy than she had in a long while.

Now though it was time to get to work again.

Chapter 11

The bedrooms were nearly ready and she and Rosanna had taken great delight in decorating them. They had always been well furnished with antiques and beautiful pictures of course as the count and his ancestors before him had always had house guests to stay, but some of the bathrooms had had antiquated plumbing which had to be updated and quite a lot of the curtains and bedding had become shabby over the years. For friends and family that had never been a problem but for a guest paying a top rate it would be. Although Rosanna had done her fair share of curtain making, they had also kept the seamstresses of the surrounding area happily busy for months.

They had taken down the most precious of the paintings for fear of damage and put them into storage. They had replaced them with less expensive but still interesting pictures of the local Tuscan countryside. Gabriella and Rosanna had taken advantage of the monthly antique fairs as well in the Piazza Grande in Arezzo to snap up bargains, going in the late afternoon of the Sunday when all the stallholders were preparing to pack up and go home and were open to being beaten down to lower prices in order to get rid of their stock. This way, they often managed to acquire some of the extra chairs they needed, small tables as well as quantities of interesting china and ornaments.

The room that Gabriella had worried about most was that of the count himself. Not because it wasn't well furnished, it was, but because it felt slightly sacrilegious to be allowing perfect strangers to sleep in her father's magnificent four-poster bed, sit on his chairs and put clothes in his wardrobe. But she reasoned, it had to be done and he would have understood. She told him all that when she paid her regular visit to his grave with Lupo, standing in the low evening sun and pouring out all her worries.

Then there was her own rather grand room which she had had to give up in order to move to a much smaller one in the attic.

"I shall have to remember that I don't sleep here anymore." She had said ruefully to Rosanna. "I will be opening the door out of force of habit and giving some poor guest a big surprise."

Rosanna had helped her sort out a multitude of childhood possessions, taking down posters of teenage crushes and bundling up books and games for charity and moving what was left up to a smaller darker room in the attic where she had a basic single bed, instead of the four-poster she was used to, a small chest of drawers, a single wardrobe and a small desk and chair. She was about to comment on this when she realised that of course it was no more than Rosanna had had for many years. She had lived up there in the room next door to Gabriella's new one and she had been the only one 'living in' so as to be near Gabriella when she was tiny. She had remained there ever since. Carmela and Antonio had a small cottage in the grounds and Tommaso lived with his wife in the nearby village.

Then they realised they would have to number the guest bedrooms.

"No, not numbers," Gabriella said after some thought, "that is too impersonal."

She mused about maybe giving them names associated with nearby Arezzo: Guido Monaco for his invention of musical notation, Vasari who wrote the biography of the artists, and maybe Saint Donatus, the patron saint of the city, but in the end, it was easier and more evocative to call them the names of the famous towns and villages of Tuscany; Florence, Sienna, Arezzo, Cortona, Lucca, San Gimignano, Pisa, Montepulciano, Volterra, Pienza, Montereggioni, and, for fun, Collodi, the 'birthplace' of Pinocchio. In that last room, they even put a puppet of Pinocchio and a copy of the story for the guests to read.

When the last nameplate had been screwed to the door by Tommaso, she and Rosanna looked at each other and sighed with satisfaction. The windows sparkled, the new bedlinen and curtains looked sumptuous and they had checked and rechecked every room endlessly to make sure nothing was out of place and each one had every facility a guest could possibly need: TVs, flasks of drinking water, tea and coffee making facilities, a hair dryer, an ironing board and an iron, bath towels, slippers, toiletries. Nothing was lacking to make a guest feel comfortable and at home.

Downstairs too was almost ready.

The main salon with its walls hung with medieval tapestries and big windows opening out onto the terrace was looking splendid. The chandeliers had been washed painstakingly piece by piece by Rosanna and Gabriella together and they sparkled brilliantly. They had stood back admiring their handiwork as Josh and Tommaso together hoisted the chandeliers carefully back into place on the vaulted ceiling. The huge open marble fireplace with its crested mantelpiece would be blazing with logs from the estate in the winter and an elegant embroidered fire screen stood in front. An enormous richly gilded mirror stood at one side reflecting the tapestry on the opposite wall. On the ceiling, there was a hunting fresco painted by Giorgio Vasari and velvet curtains were draped at the windows. In the dining room as well were new chairs and tables made from local chestnut. The huge old long table and baronial chairs that had stood there before had been placed in her father's old study ready for private functions, but for now, it was necessary to have twenty separate tables for individual guests. The bar was finished with its curve of chestnut made especially by a local craftsman and new glasses stood in serried ranks on the shelves behind. Gabriella gazed around her in satisfaction.

They would serve wine from the estate of course, but also famous Tuscan wines, Brunello di Montepulciano, full-bodied reds from the Chianti hills, Vernaccia, a dry white wine from San Gimignano, local liqueurs, Limoncello, Grappa, Fernet Branca, Amaretto. She wanted everything to be as local as possible. She had gone round all the nearby farms, asking them to grow more and sell them anything in season. The estate could supply some but they didn't have enough chickens for the quantity of eggs they would need, or the amount of fruit and vegetables. The farmers were, of course, only too eager to help. Opening day drew nearer. The local journalists, curious to see inside the Castello and also anxious to help promote the new venture, especially after a few glasses of estate wine, wrote encouragingly. TV people came and made a film which was shown on local television. Foreign journalists had stayed, sampled Carmela's cooking and written about the hotel in glowing terms. 'Quintessential Tuscany' 'A new jewel in the Tuscan hills'. Advertising in the foreign press and Italian travel magazines was paying off. Bookings started to flood in. They had taken on a few more staff ready for the opening. Two local ladies, Nella and Rosa, were to come in every morning to clean and Carmela had requested help with the dishwashing and general kitchen cleaning to free up Lucia and herself to concentrate on the cooking.

All that remained now were the guests.

Chapter 12

In the meantime, Domenico and his mother had not forgotten the conversation they had had with Gabriella. They arranged to bring a large group of their friends for an evening just before the official opening of the hotel. Gabriella had reconciled herself to seeing them. After all, she reasoned, not every hotel guest was going to be pleasant and one of the drawbacks of the job was going to be being polite to unlikeable people and she may as well start with the worst of all. Added to this, business was business and if he was prepared to pay then she was happy to take his money. They prepared an elaborate buffet and Domenico and his friends duly arrived, screeching up the drive in their expensive cars and swaggering in, treating everyone at the Castello with complete disdain. Gabriella swallowed her pride and contrived to hide her distaste for her cousin and indeed some of his friends who strode around, fingering the tapestries and stroking the furniture as well as commenting loudly on how they would have done things differently. It almost seemed that Domenico thought he owned the place, the way he was behaving. In fact, she was seething after she overheard him telling one of his friends once again, that as the nearest surviving male relative it was he who should have inherited the Castello, not Gabriella, a mere woman. He was obsessed. The group ate and drank to excess and with a sigh of relief Gabriella finally saw the last of them out of the door. Domenico reeled drunkenly towards her and she asked, "Where shall I send the account?"

"Account?" He smirked, his yellowed teeth like the fangs of a wolf, "Cara Gabriella, I have helped you by introducing future customers to your hotel. There will be no account. On the contrary, it is you who should be paying me for bringing them here." Gabriella stood open-mouthed. For a moment, she was too stunned to speak.

Then she burst out, "That is not what we agreed at all. I didn't promise anything. You booked a function for twenty people and you have to pay."

"Sue me then," said Domenico with a final sneer and flourish as he staggered drunkenly out of the door and down the front steps. Gabriella let out a howl of rage and screamed an oath at the departing figure. Josh appeared anxiously beside her on the steps.

"What's happened? What's wrong?" She collapsed sobbing.

"He won't pay. I have been taken for a fool. I should have known what he was like. How can I have been so naïve?"

"Ah," said Josh. "I was worried, knowing what you had said about his reputation. It's my fault. I am the one who should have known better. When we make a booking in future, we should always ask for a deposit. In this instance, we would have realised straight away that he had no intention of paying. I thought though, as he was your relative, he would be honourable."

"But all that food and drink we have to pay for," she hiccoughed. "And the worst of it is that all those people he brought, none of them will ever come back. They are all freeloaders, the lot of them, as mean as him."

"Well," Josh said wryly. "We've learned a valuable lesson. Let's forget about it and move on."

But it was a salutary lesson for Gabriella on the realities of running a hotel.

Chapter 13

Their first proper guests were due the following Friday and Gabriella paced restlessly all morning, checking and rechecking everything until Carmela said, "Gabriella, come and sit down in the kitchen with me. You couldn't have done anything more. Have a cup of coffee or a bowl of soup. You will be exhausted if you carry on like this." So Gabriella sat with a bowl of Carmela's minestrone and watched as she competently made her speciality 'Torta della Nonna', 'grandmother's cake', a custard flan decorated with pine nuts and sugar. It soothed Gabriella's nerves to watch her as she mixed, then rolled and cut the pastry, zested lemons, stirred custard, all while attending to what seemed like a dozen other pots and pans on the stove and giving instructions to the amiable Lucia who was preparing the vegetables. Finally, there was the sound of a car on the drive. It was a beaming Tommaso who ushered in their first guests, Mr and Mrs Fisher, a homely-looking couple from England who, she had been told, were celebrating their Golden Wedding Anniversary.

Gabriella had placed flowers and Prosecco in their room. They both exclaimed in delight when they saw the four-poster bed, the frescoed ceiling, and above all, the view from their window. Tommaso settled their bags and showed surprise at being given a tip: obviously, Gabriella smiled, he hadn't bargained on this unexpected and welcome sideline to his new job. "The dining room opens at seven, or if you would prefer to eat on the terrace, just tell us when you come down."

"Oh, is it only us?" Mrs Fisher said in surprise.

"Well," Gabriella admitted, "you are actually our first guests. The Prosecco is not just for your anniversary, we are celebrating too."

"My dear, how perfectly delightful!" Mrs Fisher clapped her hands in glee. Gabriella was waiting for them as they came down for dinner. They had elected to eat on the terrace to enjoy the sunset over the hills and it was a perfect evening. She settled them down and Josh came out from the bar with the wine they had ordered. "And this must be your lovely husband, "Mrs Fisher beamed at the pair of them. There was an awkward silence.

"I…I…" Gabriella stammered.

Josh interrupted smoothly, "I am her manager."

"Oh, I am so sorry," Mrs Fisher was flustered. "Oh, how embarrassing. It's just that you look as if …Oh, I'm making it worse…"

"No, no please, an easy mistake to make," Josh was professional, but Gabriella treasured the inference that they looked as if they belonged together as if they were a married couple…

And so it began. The hotel was open for business from that day on. It was a whirlwind of activity with each day bringing fresh challenges. It wasn't the life she had planned for herself, but then fate had decreed otherwise. She soon found that every day in the hotel business was different: good customers, bad customers, sometimes days that went wrong, but, overwhelmingly, the satisfaction of making people happy, helping them enjoy themselves. If you were gregarious and outgoing and liked people, she discovered, it was the perfect job. She might have fallen into it by accident but sometimes she thought that serendipity is indeed very much a happy accident. Above all, she loved showing off her beloved Tuscany to the visitors.

Tommaso, in his smart new minibus, drove them on every excursion and Gabriella, knowing the hotel was in safe hands with Josh, became a willing and enthusiastic tour guide. Josh had come up with the idea of selling packages to the visitors with dinner, bed and breakfast at the hotel and days spent touring the area. She took a party of guests to Cortona where she walked them through the medieval streets of the beautiful hilltop town. They sat in the square drinking coffees while Gabriella told them of its history and the fact that it had once been a papal residence. They had lunch on the terrace of a restaurant overlooking the valley, eating pasta and drinking the local wine. Then it was back to the hotel for a wonderful dinner prepared by Carmela who was now experimenting with a myriad flavours of homemade ice cream. The guests couldn't get enough of it and begged her for the recipes.

The following day, they were in Arezzo, Gabriella taking them to the old Roman Amphitheatre, the Piero frescoes that she loved in the church of San Francesco; the ancient fort at the top of the hill where she had so recently sat with Josh and from where they admired the panoramic view of the city and the surrounding countryside and of course the historic Piazza Grande. "What I can't understand," said one of the guests, "is why this place isn't better known. It's stunning."

"Ah," Gabriella laughed, "tell all your friends. Well, I love it, but then I am biased! It is much less crowded and noisy than some of the bigger cities in Italy and very safe."

"And so clean," a man commented.

"Yes, it's swept every day and the rubbish is collected every day."

He whistled in astonishment. "Tell that to our local town council in England. We only have rubbish collected once a fortnight and the streets are swept every few months if we're lucky." The following evening they were back in the city for one of the street parties held in each quarter of the city before the Joust of the Saracen that she had told Josh about or, to give it its full name in Italian the Giostra del Saracino, an ancient festival of chivalry dating back to the Middle Ages and held in Arezzo in June and September every year, with the winning quarter getting the prize of the Golden Lance. She had rung the Rettore, the Rector in charge of the quarter Santa Crucifera, who had been an old friend of her father's. In fact, many years before, she told the guests, her father, as a young man, had been a victorious rider many times in the joust. The Rettore had been delighted to hear from her and looked forward to welcoming her and her guests to the street party. On the way into the city again, Gabriella explained the history of the joust, how the four quarters competed with two riders on each side, drawn from the four original city gates, Sant'Andrea, Porta del Foro, Porta Santa Spirito and the one they were supporting, Porta Crucifera.

"Don't worry if you can't remember all the names," she said cheerfully. "Just cheer loudest for the red and green tomorrow." She also explained how each quarter had its own museum and its own social club for members, supporting the young and old alike and also taking care of anyone who needed help. There was fierce rivalry between each quarter. "You will see tomorrow how fierce," she laughed. "Cup finals in England are nothing compared to the contest here. Even husbands and wives from different quarters don't speak to each other in the weeks leading up to the joust."

They filed off the minibus outside the nearest city gate to the quarter and went under the archway with Gabriella leading the way. The guests gasped at the sight before them, with what seemed like a mile of trestle tables all laid out along the street with benches on either side. "How are they going to feed all these people?" a rather ample lady enquired, obviously worried she wasn't going to get enough to eat.

"Don't worry, you'll be amazed at how they do," Gabriella replied. They were greeted warmly by the Rettore and led to the place of honour in front of the top table where the committee sat. They sat gazing in wonder at the red and green flags draping every window in the tall buildings around them. The guests were a mixture of American, German, French and English. At first, they had nodded to each other politely but, as the wine began to flow the conversation, such as could be heard over the slogans and songs being chanted by the loyal supporters around them, grew warmer. Gabriella was amazed at how people could communicate with very little language in common. They had all been handed a red and green scarf to wear and most draped it around their necks. One lady fetchingly tied it like a ribbon around her hair, another skilfully used it as a bodice, having dashed off to find the bathroom in which to change. Everyone laughed. There were even dogs walking around wearing the colours of the quarter around their necks.

The meal was served on paper plates placed on huge wooden pallets carried by hand, one person in front, one behind, between the rows of tables. Two people carried two doled out plates. First, there was antipasto, salami, prosciutto and bruschetta, tomatoes on a slice of grilled toast and then, in no time at all, the second course, a bowl of pasta. The third course was chicken and vegetables and finally a sweet cake. A few of the guests had wandered round the back and came back to their fellow guests telling of their amazement at the efficiency of the food production. Huge vats of food which must have taken hours to prepare; about twenty people in a line each with their own job, doling out food for hundreds of people, the 'waiters', mostly the teenagers from the quarter, standing in line with their long pallets. Then, serving the food, clearing each course away and giving out the next one, all with military precision. And naturally, the wine flowed copiously. Between each course there were speeches.

Gabriella translated. Speeches of welcome for them, the guests, speeches of thanks for all those who had worked so hard to make the evening a success but, above all, speeches about the pride the quarter had in its members. The two riders who would compete for the Golden Lance were introduced amid wild cheers. Above all, there was a cry for victory, in which everyone joined, the chanting rising to a cacophony of shouting. "Sounds like a war cry," someone remarked.

"Oh, it definitely is like a war," laughed Gabriella. "Just wait until tomorrow!" The dinner was followed by dancing, the guests joining in, with more chanting and the party got wilder and wilder. Finally, Tommaso drove them all home, tired but happy.

Chapter 14

The following morning, the guests slept in and Josh had arranged a late breakfast for them when they at last ambled down. Gabriella, though, was up early and in the kitchen drinking coffee with Carmela. Josh walked in and at the sight of him, she had the usual jump of excitement which she tried hard to suppress. "Wow," he said, "I thought you'd still be asleep. I gather it was quite a wild night in town."

"Nothing compared to tonight when the winner and their entourage will be parading around the city," she laughed. Carmela was busy preparing the lunch which Josh would take with Tommaso in the minibus to the palazzo in the Piazza Grande where they would watch the joust from the private balcony with grandstand seats. Together they packed the food into refrigerated boxes, working alongside each other but trying hard not to meet each other's gaze Carmela watched the pair of them shrewdly, smiling at the sight. She had her own private thoughts, but of course, she didn't dare voice them. She shook her head slightly at the foolishness of youth. While the guests had their breakfast, Josh departed in the minibus to set things up at the palazzo while Gabriella waited for a few latecomers who decided to miss breakfast for the sake of an extra hour's lie-in. She had arranged snacks for the minibus when Tommaso brought it back after leaving Josh. So they wouldn't starve! "First of all," she said, "I will take you back to Porta Crucifera to show you the horses and riders being blessed in their own church. Oh and don't be worried when you hear cannon fire. It marks all the significant moments of the day. There was one at 7 am."

"Thank goodness we didn't hear that; it would really not have helped my hangover," remarked one of the latecomers, and everyone laughed.

"And the next cannon shot will be at eleven when they bless the horses."

"Do you mean the horses get taken into the church too?" Someone asked incredulously. Indeed they did, the riders and their entourages dressed in chain mail arriving in a rush of excitement from the onlookers, removing their helmets as a gesture of respect, then dismounting and leading their horses into the church to be blessed by the priest.

"Wow," said one of the guests, "I can't get over the feeling I've gone back a few centuries with all these ancient buildings and everyone dressed in these costumes." They could already hear war-like drumming and the sound of bugles as the bands were assembling. Then Gabriella shepherded them on through the crowds to a vantage point near the cathedral where at two o'clock there was a further cannon shot, the signal for all the quarters to combine and in they came, congregating from all four parts of the city, lords and ladies in their velvet finery, crossbowmen and warriors carrying pikes, the captains and officials of each quarter on brightly caparisoned horses. It was a magnificent sight. Group by group, they marched along, ranging themselves in long lines along the wide steps of the cathedral.

Finally, there was a silence, pregnant with anticipation; the side gate of the Duomo opened and the bishop appeared in all his solemnity. The entire contingent was blessed, the drumming began again in earnest and then the procession moved off round the city where excited crowds who hadn't been able to get tickets for the joust itself were gathered, lining the streets with small children sitting on parent's shoulders. It was a sea of waving flags on all sides, including high up from the open windows and balconies of many of the apartments where people crowded, even the rooftops where some were perched precariously. "What happens now?" Someone asked.

"Now we go to the house in the square and have lunch."

"Oh good," said the ample lady, "I'm starving." They entered the square and pushed their way through the crowds and despite the serried ranks of metal seats ready for the spectators which obscured some of the lower parts of the buildings, it was still impressive and her guests looked around them in awe. She led them to a door on the far side which she unlocked and they filed inside the cool hallway. "We're at the top," she explained. "Don't worry, we have a lift." She had looked at the apprehensive faces of some of them after their long walk in the sun, thinking they had to climb steep flights of stairs.

Josh was waiting for them on the top floor with welcoming glasses of freshly squeezed lemon juice loaded with ice and glasses of wine. Some of the guests wasted no time in going outside on the balcony. "What a view," they exclaimed. They were looking across at the curved back of the Pieve, the ancient abbey, the Tribunale with its clock face and the loggia at the top of the square. The sand strip, the Lizza, up which the riders would gallop, started near them at the bottom and continued diagonally up to the top of the square. At this point stood a model of a Saracen, on the arm of which the target would be placed.

"It's called the Buratto the King of the Indies. The joust goes back to the time of the Crusades," Gabriella said. "But it's just symbolic now in case you think it's not politically correct," she finished wryly. "The joust started as a military exercise, a training for knights, but evolved into the pageant we have today." She explained that each rider galloped up the strip of sand holding a lance and had to hit the target, scoring between one and five points depending on which part he hit.

"Oh, you mean they don't fight each other?" One guest said in disappointment.

"No they don't, but I guarantee you'll find it exciting just the same. I've seen the joust hundreds of times and each time I love it. As I've said, my father used to be one of the riders."

"And did he win?"

"Yes, he was one of the most successful riders of all time," she said proudly. "Sadly he is no longer with us."

"Oh, that's a shame." Gabriella was aware of Josh watching her but she carried on.

"It's a test of skill. The lances are very heavy, held in one hand while you are controlling the reins of the horse with the other at full gallop. Added to which, if you look carefully, there are mental balls on chains attached to the Saracen's arm. If you ride too slowly the arm will swing around and the balls will knock you off your horse. And even if they don't, the balls have black powder on them which will mark your costume so the judges will know and deduct points."

"Wow," one of the guests exclaimed. "Nasty." They left the balcony and went inside and Josh helped everyone to lunch. It was crowded in the room and several times they brushed against each other. Her cheeks were burning but she hoped the guests would put it down to the heat. Lunch finished, some of the guests lingered on the balcony; others took advantage of the comfortable sofas. A few took it further and were having a quiet nap, exhausted by the excitement of the morning and indeed the night before. She and Josh cleared away and as the drumming grew nearer, they gathered the guests together. The square was rapidly filling up with chanting supporters, corralled in sections at the corners to separate them from each other. The doorbell rang and Gabriella and Josh grinned at each other knowing what was about to happen. Josh opened the door while Gabriella politely asked the guests to leave the balcony. They were reluctant to go and some protested, until they saw the advancing group of buglers processing in their colourful red and cream uniforms through the sitting room.

"It has always been a tradition that the buglers signal the beginning of the joust from this balcony," Gabriella explained.

"Great, awesome," several people remarked. The buglers took their positions on the balcony and the clarion call to arms sounded across the square. The imposing figure of the Maestro del Campo, the Master of the Field, announced the beginning of the proceedings. Then the procession began. The guests, having taken selfies with the buglers before they left to take their place in the square, hurried back onto the balcony. It was spectacular. Each quarter with its knights on horseback, its soldiers and its bands slowly entered and the drumming grew intense. They took their allotted places at the back of the square, then it was the turn of the Bandieri, the flag bearers, who gave a display, tossing and waving their huge flags on heavy wooden poles in an almost balletic display. Her guests were enchanted. Then the two riders for each quarter were introduced to boos and cheers depending on which quarter the supporters were allied to, and the real battle began. There were police in the square in case things got out of hand. "Which they often do," Gabriella conceded with a grin. The first horse bearing the pink and gold colours of Porto del Foro came through the barrier and was skittish because of the crowds and the noise. The rider fought to control it while the lance was brought slowly down from the top of the square and handed to him by a man on horseback.

"They don't bring their own?"

"No, each lance must be exactly like the others to avoid any possible advantage," she explained. The crowd yelled as he took off at last at a fast gallop, the lance pointing towards the target. There was a bang as the lance hit the target and the supporters near him let out a scream of joy. They had obviously seen the score. The two costumed attendants in Turkish garb detached the target and rushed it to the red-robed judges sitting high on their stand under the loggia. "It's a knockout competition," Gabriella explained. "The target is divided into areas with, of course, five being the bull. The two riders' scores are added together and if two or more quarters get the same score they ride again." There was a long pause as the target was scrutinised and then a messenger hurried to the Master of the Field. Slowly, building the tension, came the announcement, "The first rider of Porto del Foro has scored" ... he raised his voice before pronouncing dramatically, "Five points."

There were screams of ecstasy from the supporters; howls of rage and scorn from their enemies. And so it continued with the first of each quarter scoring. The loudest screams from the guests, who were getting fully immersed in the proceedings, were of course for Porta Crucifera. " Are they all men...the riders I mean?" One of the women asked.

"Yes, traditionally," replied Gabriella.

"Well, I guess if the lance is heavy I suppose a woman couldn't handle it."

"I'm sure if a woman had a bit of training she could. It's not the weight, it's the way you hold it. I used to hold my father's lance sometimes when I was young."

"Well," said the first woman. "If your father used to compete in the joust, I'm sure you could have a go. I saw you out on your horse the other day and you are quite the rider."

"Thank you," Gabriella laughed but she caught Josh looking at her with an amused smile. The next rider scored four points, and after that, it was all over as the second rider for Porta del Foro also scored five points, making an unbeatable ten. Their supporters went wild and mobbed the rider with the police desperately trying to keep control as the prize of the Golden Lance was presented. Despite their disappointment at Porta Crucifera not winning, the guests loved it all. "That was one of the most spectacular and colourful things I've ever seen," one sighed as they made their way downstairs and into the square to board the minibus to return to the hotel for one of Carmela's very special dinners. They had to fight their way through the crowds of supporters for Porta del Foro streaming en masse behind their horses and riders to the Duomo for the triumphant ceremony of giving thanks for their victory, accompanied by the drummers. It had been a long and tiring day and it was two o'clock in the morning before Gabriella's head sank gratefully onto her pillow. She awoke suddenly at five am with one thought in her head. Why couldn't the rider be a girl?

Why not indeed?

Chapter 15

She should have known it was too good to last.

Everything had been going so well.

The day after the trip to the joust, Gabriella stood at the front door of the Castello waving off the last guests to leave. Several of them had vowed to come back as she had promised more guided tours to some of the wonderful places Tuscany had to offer. She was buzzing with excitement and her mind leapt ahead. Wine tours to villages like Montepulciano with its excellent vintages in ancient cellars carved out of volcanic rock, some of them on foundations of old Etruscan tombs: art tours for the frescoes of Piero Della Francesca both in Arezzo and the villages and towns where his other famous works were, including his home town of San Sepulcro; gastronomic tours for the Sagras, the food festivals held in every town and village in the autumn. The list was endless.

A moment later, the bubble burst.

Josh came towards her with a serious expression on his face. "We have a problem," he said gravely

"What's the matter?" Gabriella was alarmed. "Is it one of the staff?"

"No, they're all ok. I've just had a call from one of our wine suppliers. He says we owe him 2000 euros."

"What! But I thought our payments were all up to date?"

"Exactly, I've been through the books carefully. I then rang him back saying there must be some mistake and he told me your cousin Domenico had ordered a large consignment of wine to be sent to his address and that you had authorised it."

Gabriella turned white. "How dare he!" she spluttered "Who does he think he is?"

She raced inside and grabbed her phone frantically punching in his number.

"Pronto?" Domenico's voice drawled.

Gabriella couldn't speak for a few moments, she was so incensed. She took a few deep breaths to calm herself. "Domenico, I have just been told you have ordered a large amount of wine and put it on our account. I don't remember authorising you to do that."

" Oh," he said casually. "I didn't think you'd mind. After all, we are family and you get a trade discount, don't you? You are obviously doing well so I thought you'd be happy to support your poor relations."

"I suppose," she raged, "there is no point in asking you to pay or to give us the wine, but I want to warn you that I am contacting every one of our suppliers this week and telling them that they are not to accept orders from anyone except those authorised by myself or Josh."

There was silence at the end of the line.

"Well, if your boyfriend is more important than your family so be it," he drawled, "but I warn you I can make things exceedingly unpleasant for you among our friendship group. Rumours of failure and bad practice can be spread very easily."

"You just try," Gabriella almost shouted, "I think most decent people will know what a conniving, slimy creature you are and will ignore everything you say."

There was a further silence at the other end of the line, then the call broke off with a click.

She stood fuming, her heart racing.

"Wow," said Josh, "that was really telling him."

She looked at him helplessly. "I suppose we'll have to pay it," she said resignedly, "the wine has gone and probably nearly all consumed by now. The supplier should have checked but he took the order in good faith."

She longed to race across the room and throw herself into his arms for comfort, but she didn't dare.

"I'm going out for a while, sorry, Josh," was all she said instead.

She raced past him out to the stables, Lupo after her. Tosca was still in her stall and she saddled her quickly. The horse sensing her agitation was skittish at first but as Gabriella swung herself into the saddle she responded. They trotted across the grounds of the Castello and out onto the lowlands of the Apennines. Leaning forward, she urged Tosca into a gallop and the three of them, the dog behind, raced across the fields, heedless of danger.

Nothing soothed her like riding her horse and Tosca responded as girl and horse moved as one. Gabriella screamed into the wind, venting all her rage and frustration to no one but the open sky and the hills.

When they returned an hour later, she felt a little better. She swung out of the saddle, lifted it off the horse's back and gave her a long drink of water. She rubbed the horse down and led her back into her stall.

Josh was waiting as she went back inside.

"Feeling better?" He said ruefully

"Well," Gabriella said, "I could still murder him, but we have work to do. We must make sure that he can't do anything like that again."

She was trying to sound brisk and efficient when all she wanted to do was grab hold of him and kiss him.

They stood gazing at each other for a long moment before he said, "Alright, I'll get onto it right away."

He turned and walked to the office while she went into the kitchen where Carmela was making Aroncini, pear-shaped rice cakes. She made herself a double espresso and snaffled some of the leftover mixture just as she used to do when she was a child. Carmela made a 'pretend' slap at her hand in return, smiling as she did so.

"Everyone complimented you on your delicious meals," Gabriella said.

"That's good," Carmela was pleased.

Then she looked at Gabriella's face. "Everything alright?"

"No, not really," Gabriella replied. She told Carmela what Domenico had been up to.

"Mascalzone! What a bad man." Carmela was shocked. "That side of the family has never been any good. Your father hated them."

At the mention of her father, Gabriella suddenly burst into floods of tears. Carmela, sticky hands notwithstanding wiped her hands on her apron and moved swiftly to enfold Gabriella in her motherly bosom. She stroked Gabriella's hair and spoke soothingly to her.

"Oh, I miss him so much," Gabriella sobbed. "He was just always there, Carmela. How could he have left me like this?"

Carmela held her until the sobs subsided.

"Mia Cara, my darling, it will be alright you will see. You are such a good girl, stronger than you think, like your father. He would be so proud of you, of what you are doing."

"Thank you," Gabriella said eventually with a final shuddering sob. She went to the kitchen sink and splashed her face with water. "Now I must get back to work. Thank heavens I have Josh to help."

"Yes indeed," Carmela said with a meaningful look. "That young man is worth his weight in gold. What would you do without him?"

Chapter 16

As usual, Carmela was busy in the kitchen when Gabriella popped in for a quick coffee.

"That smells good," she commented, lifting the lid of the saucepan simmering on the stove.

"Salsa de lepre," Carmela said.

Hare sauce was a rich accompaniment for the wide strips of pappardelle pasta that Lucia had been busy making, rolling and cutting assiduously. The sauce was rich with herbs and spices. It was a time of plenty in the kitchen with the gardeners bringing in fresh produce every day. Carmela and Lucia could hardly keep up with a constant supply of courgettes, artichokes, aubergines, figs and chestnuts together with apples and pears from the orchard and of course fragrant lemons and oranges. They had bottled, preserved and frozen cherries, apricots and other soft fruit and made an endless supply of fresh tomato sauce flavoured with basil and oregano.

Some of the guests asked for typical Tuscan dishes and were often surprised when they were told they could have Papa al Pomodoro, a tomato dish made simply of bread, tomato, garlic and basil, or ribollita, a stew of cabbage, beans, onions and carrots. Gabriella had to explain that much of the traditional Tuscan food was peasant food based on what people had been able to afford in the past.

"Tuscans," she explained to amused guests, "are known as bean eaters because they eat so many, including dishes like pasta and bean soup or pasta with beans. Our typical bread is just yeast, water and flour with no salt because our food is so spicy and we have oil with our bread, not butter. But," she continued looking at a few crestfallen faces "we also have wild boar sauce and salami, porchetta, which is a pork dish stuffed with rosemary, sage, garlic and wild fennel, roasted guinea fowl and wonderful desserts, of course, such as castanachio, a rich chestnut cake, bombolone which are like doughnuts filled with jam, chocolate or cream then panforte, a thick cake of nuts, candied fruit, honey and spices. And of course, cheeses. Our best local cheese is pecorino made of sheep's milk."

"I'm putting on weight just listening to you," one woman laughed.

"And gelato don't forget the gelato," said her husband grinning broadly, "so many different flavours. Your chef is amazing."

"It's a woman, Carmela," Gabriella said. "I'll introduce you and you can tell her yourself, she'll be delighted."

But the pride of Tuscan cooking and the thing that most people wanted to taste was of course the truffle.

Tommaso had come into the kitchen one day saying to Carmela, "I have something really special for you."

He produced from his pocket a tiny carefully wrapped parcel. To the naked eye, it looked like a little piece of dirt but to Carmela, it looked as if he had found a nugget of gold.

"Madonna!" she exclaimed. It was a small but beautiful truffle. So the guests dined on pasta scented with truffle that night.

"Wow, that was exquisite," said the man who loved gelato, mopping every scrap of sauce with his bread.

Gabriella explained that Tommaso, the hotel driver and handyman had picked it up the previous night while out walking with his dog.

"I'd love to see how they are found," the man said.

"Well, I'll see what I can do," said Gabriella glancing at Josh who nodded approvingly. "Many truffle hunters go out at night, afraid that other hunters will spot them and steal their booty but I am sure Tommaso would be willing to take you during the day."

Several of the other guests were listening eagerly and asked to come as well. So early the next morning, a proud Tommaso and his faithful hound Cicero lead a keen group of guests wearing sturdy footwear out into the woods. He didn't speak much English or German and there were several of each nationality in the group so Josh had volunteered to go along as well to translate. Gabriella, not to be left out, put on a warm jacket and boots and accompanied them. Lupo, sadly, had to be left at the hotel because Cicero was the dog of the moment and Lupo would only have got in the way.

Tommaso, with Josh translating, explained as they went along and Gabriella, as usual, was surprised at how much Josh knew as well. Or perhaps she shouldn't have been surprised: he was knowledgeable about most things it seemed.

"I used to go out with my uncle in my teens when I was on holiday here," he explained. They were walking along behind the group and several times, because the ground was slippery and uneven in places, they ended up almost touching and once he held her hand as he helped her down a slope. Their eyes met and he looked hastily away.

"A truffle," Josh translated, "is the fruit of a kind of fungus found at the base of a tree among the roots. They used to be much more readily available but are now much rarer, so therefore are much more expensive."

Tommaso went on, "There are different kinds of truffles associated with different trees, some more perfumed than others. In Italy, we used to hunt truffles with pigs but since 1985 they have been forbidden in Italy because they do so much damage to the mycelia which form the fungus and also because they eat the truffles themselves. So," concluded Tomasso proudly, "I have trained Cicero here to hunt for them."

They were now deep into the woods and at the very moment, he spoke, Cicero's nose lifted and twitched and then he began to dig furiously at the base of a nearby tree. Tommaso bent down and used his fingers to delve between the tree roots then raised his hand triumphantly holding a small nobbly truffle.

"Doesn't look much, does it?" One of the guests said.

"Ah, just wait until you taste it," said Josh.

They all trooped back to the Castello to change their shoes and then they were all invited into the kitchen to meet Carmela.

She was in her element. She was making a chicken for that night and they watched attentively as she shaved the truffle finely, being careful not to waste a morsel, and inserted some of the shavings under the skin of the chicken. After she had put it in the oven, she used some of the rest to make chocolate truffles for dessert.

Tommaso of course was paid handsomely for his finds and Gabriella and Josh were equally well rewarded with happy guests. They exchanged satisfied looks with each other.

"We must do that again," he whispered. "The guests love it."

"Definitely," she said, but of course, much as she had enjoyed the truffle hunt, she had enjoyed walking with him and being so close to him even more, savouring the memory of his hand in hers.

Chapter 17

The Christmas market in Arezzo was in full swing. Brightly lit stalls filled the Piazza Grande. Every year the stallholders came down from the Tyrol in the southern Alps and there was mulled wine, sausages, cheeses of all kinds and pastries such as apple strudel. Added to this, the monthly antique market for which Arezzo was famous and which normally took place in the piazza, had spilt out onto the park under the fortress at the top of the hill and onto the main Corso and side streets so that the whole city was buzzing.

Gabriella had taken her latest group of guests to see the festivities and to do some shopping. Once again they used the house on the piazza as a focal point with refreshments and drinks. Some hardy souls sat out on the balcony in near-freezing temperatures and Gabriella had provided blankets for them, but most were inside in the warm.

Several of them had remarked that they didn't realise Italy got so cold in the winter

"Sadly yes," Gabriella replied, "we are up in the hills and the more north you are, the colder Italy gets, but you can see it's a crisp cold."

Mrs Fisher, their very first guest had returned with her husband to do her Christmas shopping.

"Such a lovely view looking down on the square," she said closing the French windows behind her to keep out the cold as she came back into the room, "and even the buildings are lit up with images of cascading stars. I love the history of the place, the abbey and the other building…what did you call it?"

"The Tribunale. It used to be the old law court. In a minute the choir will be out from the music school over the loggia."

Just as she spoke, she could see them filing out onto the steps of the Tribunale and they all went out onto the balcony again, leaning on the rail and listening entranced to wonderful Christmas songs, sung by classical singers.

"It's all so magical," Mrs Fisher clapped her hands in glee as finally the choir finished and left the steps. But her attention was soon deflected to the most important matter of the day, "and the shopping, all those lovely leather goods," she went on, "I'm buying all my Christmas presents here. Handbags for the girls, daughters, daughters-in-law, granddaughters…and wallets and man bags for the boys."

"I can take you around and show you the best shops. There's someone who makes all his own leather goods," Gabriella offered. "Then if you like, your husband can relax here."

She saw Mr Fisher glance at her gratefully.

"Oh, that would be lovely. And I still do Christmas stockings for everyone. I can browse the markets afterwards for trinkets."

"Steady on," laughed her husband, "We will need a pantechnicon to get home"

"But that's why I came with an extra empty suitcase," she replied smugly.

Once the singing was over, it was time to move. The guests wove their way through the crowds. The group dispersed to browse among the stalls. Gabriella asked them to be back at the house by five.

Normally, most shops closed in the afternoon in Italy but in the lead-up to Christmas, they took advantage of the extra trade and stayed open. She spied several of the guests already enjoying the mulled wine and another at one of the antique stalls bargaining for an old map of the city. She hoped the suspension on the minibus would hold up after all these purchases.

She took Mrs Fisher to the shop with the handmade leather goods. It seemed to take an age with Mrs Fisher dithering over the size and colour of each bag and endlessly consulting her list to make sure she hadn't left anyone out. Finally, they were done and Gabriella managed to get her a good discount for the vast quantity she had bought, leaving a delighted owner and an equally delighted Mrs Fisher.

They left the shop loaded with shopping bags. On the way back, she almost cannoned into Cara, her face layered with even more panstick make-up in a vain effort to look young and her hair still stiff with spray.

"My dear Gabriella," she oozed. "Domenico has told me of your generosity over the wine. We are so grateful and I hope you won't forget us over Christmas, a time to give gifts to all, including your poor relations."

If Mrs Fisher hadn't been there, Gabriella would have been tempted to be rude but she bit her lip and tried hard to keep her temper.

"How could I possibly forget you?" She said in the sweetest manner she could muster. "You have been on my mind constantly. Now if you will forgive me I have guests to attend to."

The sarcasm was of course lost on Cara and Gabriella turned swiftly away and led Mrs Fisher back towards the square. Luckily, her guest was too enraptured with her purchases to notice anything amiss.

Josh came to help carry all their bags upstairs and Mr Fisher decided to join his wife browsing in the square so Gabriella and Josh were alone.

"Stiff drink?" He said looking at her face once the Fishers had departed and she could stop being the perfect hostess for a moment.

" Better not," Gabriella said ruefully. "I don't want to appear tiddly in front of the guests though I'm sorely tempted." She told him about the encounter with Cara. "Totally shameless they are, the pair of them."

He frowned. "They are obviously going to be an ongoing problem. We'll have to think of a strategy to cope with them and be extra vigilant in case they try anything like the wine fraud again. I've already made the situation quite clear to all the suppliers."

"But what can we do?" Gabriella was in despair. "They are like angry wasps on a pot of jam, busy circling until they spot an opportunity and dive in. Nothing short of actually swatting them will deter them."

"Quite," Josh said, "sadly swatting people is illegal."

He smiled at her. "Come and sit down for a bit."

He patted the sofa beside him and she did as she was told.

They sat in companionable silence for a few moments, their shoulders almost touching. He was so easy to be with, Gabriella thought, so calm and soothing. That was why he was so good at his job. Nothing seemed to faze him.

Or did it? The fact that she had a title and owned the Castello had thrown him. And was it entirely by accident, one of those one-in-a-million chances that made him apply for this job? Or did he really pursue her all the way to Italy after one magical moment on a train? The questions hung in the air and she did not dare to say anything for fear of embarrassment.

Or perhaps she should say something.

She made up her mind. She was going to ask him.

She opened her mouth to speak but at that precise moment, one of the guests rang the doorbell and so it was time to gather them all together and board the minibus for home.

And the opportunity was lost.

Chapter 18

Christmas was spent with a houseful of guests, blazing fires, chestnuts gathered from the trees on the estate, good local wine and cheeses such as pecorino from the milk of local ewes. There was an abundance of Porcini mushrooms that had been picked locally and dried by Carmela and Lucia in the autumn and which were now made into delicious risottos. Afterwards, they ate panettone and panforte, cakes of which the guests couldn't get enough. The Christmas markets were still in full swing and windows were full of nativity scenes and lighted candles.

Gabriella told her guests all about Christmas traditions in Italy. "Babbo Natale, Father Christmas brings the presents for children, but they also get presents from the Befana, an old witch who comes at Epiphany, the 6th of January, echoing the journey of the Wise Men visiting Jesus."

"Lucky kids," said one visiting American. "Glad my grandkids don't know that or they'll all want to move to Italy." Gabriella and Josh had put up a tree together, standing side by side as she handed him the decorations to hang on the highest branches, their fingers touching as they did so. She had bitten her lip hard to quell the emotion that had arisen in her and she noted that he was trying hard not to look at her, just reaching down his hand for the next bauble. She had also put out, as was the custom, her own precious nativity scene that had been handed down through generations of her family, hoping that none of the guests would break it. As she had arranged the last piece she had stood back in satisfaction. "Buon Natale Papa, Buon Natale Mamma, Happy Christmas," she whispered. It was another Christmas without her father and pangs of grief overwhelmed her once more, remembering how she had put up the decorations with her father every year, him standing on the step ladder as Josh was now, with her handing them up.

She had gifts for all the staff, warm shawls for the two older women, wine for the men and money for the younger members of the staff. New Year, or San

Silvestro, went swimmingly too, with a magnificent dinner for the guests served up by Carmela and fireworks to follow, organised by Antonio. Gabriella amused them with stories of Tuscan New Year traditions. "Eating lentils at midnight brings good luck and you must have twelve grapes, one for each month of the year to come. Also, I hope you all have your lucky red underpants on but not the ones you bought yourself. They must have been given to you as a gift. It is lucky that we are not down in the city because it is a particularly dangerous night of the year when people throw old things out of the window to symbolise a fresh start, even their furniture, and you wouldn't want to be hit by a flying sofa."

At one point, she saw Josh standing temptingly under a bough of mistletoe and moved nearer to him to risk giving him a kiss, but at the last moment a guest called him and he moved so the moment of opportunity was lost. By the time the last guest left, she was exhausted. There had never been a moment to relax and she had discovered how tiring it was being perpetually smiling and pleasant to the guests, never letting them see that perhaps your feet hurt or you were longing to sit down for a moment and shut your eyes. Not that the guests had been anything but wonderful, but every detail had had to be checked a dozen times to make sure everything went smoothly.

They had no one booked in until the sixth of January so she allowed herself the luxury of a lie-in the next day. But maybe exhaustion had something to do with what followed. Later that morning she went into the kitchen. It was empty. No Carmela. She frowned. Usually, Carmela was up with the lark, singing as she prepared breakfasts, then the doughs for both the bread and the fresh pasta she made every day. Was she ill? Eventually, Lucia appeared. "Buongiorno Lucia," Gabriella said, "Where's Carmela?"

"Oh, didn't you know? She's taking her holiday. Josh told her to take a week's leave because she worked so hard over Christmas and New Year."

"Oh yes, of course, I'd forgotten," Gabriella bluffed quickly. She raced out of the kitchen to find Josh who was in the office sorting through some accounts. "Did you give Carmela the week off?"

"Yes, why? Is that a problem?" He looked at her quizzically. "She needs to rest. I just thought that we were very quiet for a week or two now and she's been working very hard recently. Lucia is quite capable of stepping in for a while."

"Yes, of course, I understand that, but you didn't think to ask me first?"

"Well," he said, looking slightly confused, "I am your manager and I thought I was allowed to make those sorts of decisions." It was then that Gabriella made her fatal mistake. All the tension between them that she had felt over the past months, trying to resist telling him how she felt about him, suddenly overwhelmed her.

"Well, in case you had forgotten, I own this place and I am the one to make those sorts of decisions around here. You are just my employee," she snapped. The moment the words were out of her mouth, she was appalled at herself. Tears sprang into her eyes as she realised she had been a complete and utter fool. It was by far the worst thing she had ever said in her life and there was no way of unsaying it. The damage was done. He had first gone white, then flushed red and gazed back at her with the strangest expression on his face. "I'm sorry," she spluttered, "I didn't mean that."

"No," he retorted, "maybe you didn't, but it just goes to show you consider me the hired help around here, one of your servants and if I mean no more to you than that I will give you my resignation today. I will stay until you find a replacement or I can leave today. Whatever you wish."

"Josh," she said, "please, I'm sorry." But it was too late. He had turned on his heels and gone, leaving her staring despairingly after him, knowing how much she relied on him. And also how much she was in love with him.

Chapter 19

So Gabriella did what she always did when she needed solace. She went riding. Firstly though she left a note, once more apologising and asking him to reconsider or at least to stay until she found a replacement. She needed a distraction from the situation with Josh and she knew exactly what that distraction would be. The seed that had been planted when she took her guests to the joust had been at the back of her mind for some time and now was the time to act on it. She took Tosca out to the flattest field she could find, far from the Castello. She didn't want anyone seeing her and wondering what on earth she was up to. First, she found a long branch the approximate weight and length of a lance, over three metres, and held it in her hand. She was shocked at how difficult it was, to get the weight and the length balanced. She held it about a metre in with two metres in front until she judged it was correct. But it was still awkward: and that was only when she was standing on firm ground, not on horseback. She wasn't sure how to introduce the concept to Tosca either: having a long pole suddenly in her field of vision might spook her. She decided to start with a smaller pole. She would also be riding with only one hand on the reins, so the distribution of her weight on the horse would be different. There were so many things to consider.

Slowly, slowly, she mounted Tosca and tried riding with a short pole. The mare was, as she had expected, uneasy at first and kept turning left as if trying to get away from the pole on her right side impeding her eyesight. Then gradually she could feel the horse adjusting to the new distribution of weight. She was a good and patient filly and the horse and rider had trusted each other for so long that she knew Gabriella wouldn't do anything to harm her.

She remembered when she had returned to Italy when her father died and how Tosca seemed to want to console her in her grief, nuzzling her and whickering softly as Gabriella had sobbed into her neck.

Every morning for the next few weeks, she rose early, gradually increasing the length of the pole until she reached the full size. That, she discovered, was only the start. It was all very well getting used to holding a long pole in one hand but you also had to hold it so well and aim it so exactly at a small target while you were at full gallop. She set a makeshift target up on a branch of a dead tree and tried endlessly to aim at it, hoping against hope that one day she would hit the bull. At first, she couldn't even make contact with the target, let alone the magic centre, but she was nothing if not determined and gradually, gradually, she persevered until one day, she exulted as, at last, she finally made contact with the target. Not the centre, that would be asking too much, but she was getting there. Tosca too seemed to have now got used to the routine and whinnied every morning when she arrived as if to say, 'Come along, let's get on with it.'

But riding Tosca was only a partial distraction from the situation with Josh and once she had finished her ride every day she still had to face him. She tried apologising again but he stonily ignored her apologies, just saying that he needed time to think. There was plenty to do even if they had no guests staying, preparing for the next season. From Easter onwards, due to Josh's astute marketing, they were almost completely fully booked. Nothing more has been said about him leaving but he had asked very pointedly for some time off, citing the fact that his mother and father were coming to visit his aunt near Assisi, an hour and a half away, but she secretly wondered if he was also taking the time to apply for another position. The atmosphere had been impossibly tense and they had spent the last weeks avoiding each other wherever possible. She couldn't bear it if he went.

It would be bad enough from the work point of view. She had grown used to relying on his sound judgement and management skills to run the hotel smoothly, but even worse, from a personal point of view she was devastated. How could she have been so stupid? She raged at herself. Fool! Fool! Up until now, he had driven the hotel minibus, but now he had hired a small Fiat and on the day he was due to depart, she stood miserably at the window watching him load his bag into the boot. He made to get into the driver's seat but at the very last minute, he looked up. She tried to withdraw but she wasn't quite quick enough. He half raised his hand in salutation and she, after a moment's hesitation, did the same. Then he was gone.

Chapter 20

She turned away from the window at last, as his car finally disappeared from view down the long drive of cypress trees and through the wrought iron gates, straining to get the last glimpse of him. Then she turned and picked up a cushion and in a fury, she pummelled her fists into it as hard as she could. She went down into the kitchen where Carmela, back from her holiday, was once again reigning supreme. Gabriella found her sitting at the large kitchen table busily drawing up menus for the new season. They sat and drank coffee together while they discussed the meals they would serve, what would be in season that they would have on the estate or what they could buy locally. Gabriella couldn't remember a time without Carmela's comforting presence. While Rosanna was wiry and energetic, it was often to Carmela that Gabriella went to curl up and be enveloped in the warmth of her ample bosom. Not that she could do that now of course even if she had wanted to. She was far too old. Carmela was very tactful and, sensing Gabriella's mood, she approached the subject delicately. "So he's gone then?"

"Who? Oh, Josh, yes, he deserves a break," she said in pretend carelessness.

"You'll miss him."

"Oh yes, of course. There's plenty to do."

"Um," Carmela began tentatively. "Is everything alright between you? I mean you don't have to tell me if you don't want to, but I've been sensing an atmosphere."

"Oh, Carmela!" Gabriella burst out. "I've been so stupid, so utterly stupid." She couldn't tell Carmela the real reason for the row as it was about her. "We had a quarrel about something, something really trivial and I was way out of order with him, overbearing and bossy." She couldn't look Carmela in the eye, she was so ashamed. Carmela waited.

"I think I more or less, in fact, more than less, told him he was my employee and should do as he was told, which he is technically but it was not the right thing to say at all."

"Ah," Carmela said gently, "no, perhaps not. But I think he is perhaps a little more than that."

Gabriella looked at her. "Is it so obvious?"

Carmela laughed. "The tension between the two of you could set the house on fire. It reminds me of when your father met your mother and the sparks that flew then. He chased her desperately but she was determined not to be caught too easily even though it was obvious that she wanted him. Then it was your father sitting here at the table moaning that she wouldn't give an inch." Gabriella told her what had happened on the train in London while Carmela sat amazed. "Cara mia, that is amazing. So it was meant to be. It is not a coincidence that he came here then?"

"But we never speak of it," Gabriella said.

"Why ever not?"

"Because I didn't want to be the first one to speak, maybe to embarrass myself."

"And he is thinking the same thing, so it's an impasse with neither of you wanting to be the first to say something…Ah, the stubbornness of youth," she smiled wryly.

"But there's more," Gabriella continued. "I think maybe he did come here on an impulse but my friend Flick didn't tell him I owned the Castello or that I had a title and I think he is now worried that he would be accused of social climbing or chasing me for my title and my supposed money, though he knows the financial state we are in now. He appears to have come from a very humble background, his aunt has a small farm near Assisi and he has gone there now. Oh, Carmela, what happens if he decides to leave? How will I bear it?" And she burst into tears again and sobbed as if her heart would break, not even calmed by Carmela moving forward to envelop her in her arms and hold her tightly, stroking her hair and muttering soothing words just as if she were a small child again who had hurt her knee.

Chapter 21

It was the longest week of her life until he returned. She rode Tosca, she practised with her pole, she went for long walks, she paced the Castello looking for problems to solve; she polished furniture that had already been polished. She hardly slept. Finally, finally, her heart leapt at the sound of his car coming up the drive. After that moment of joy, she was suddenly full of fear. What would happen if, when he came through the door, he announced his intention of leaving? She pretended to be busy polishing a mirror in the hallway even though Nella, one of the cleaners, had thoroughly dusted it that morning. "Oh hello, you're back." She tried to sound casual. "Did you have a good time? Was everyone well…your parents? Your aunt and uncle?"

"I did thank you and yes, everyone is well," his answer was equally polite and distant. He obviously wasn't going to elaborate. "I'll just go and unpack and then you can give me my…" he hesitated. He was obviously going to be sarcastic and say 'orders' but then thought better of it. "You can fill me in on what's been happening." He moved towards the stairs, ready to go up to his room in the attic, ironically the old staff quarters.

"Josh," she said quietly. He stopped, his back to her, stiff with pride. "Please forgive me. I don't why I said what I did. I was tired I think and surprised at not finding Carmela in the kitchen and having Lucia tell me something I should have known already. I was extremely stupid and reacted badly."

He stood motionless for a while, then he turned. His face was serious. "Gabriella, I don't know what to say. I thought we were getting on so well, that you treated me as an equal, professionally speaking, that is. I know you are far above me in social standing and I would never presume to equal you on that score, but I do know my job and I thought you trusted me to do it."

"I do, really I do. I can only repeat what I said and I am more sorry than I can say." She suddenly found herself becoming heated again and tried to control her tone, "As for social standing, why would I have wanted to turn this place into a hotel if I had enough money to keep it going privately? You know as well as I do that I will lose it if I don't succeed. The bank will take it over. As for my title, that is meaningless in today's world. Nearly all the so-called aristocracy are struggling to stay afloat, saddled with huge ancient buildings that they don't have the money to keep up."

"Nevertheless," he retorted, "you are entitled and used to having servants. However much you protest that they are your friends, they never will be really. They still rely on you for their wages and your goodwill. You could still dismiss them tomorrow." His tone was icy cold and his expression the same. She could see, finally, how deep the hurt had gone.

"Josh, please don't go. Please," she was pleading now.

"You know," he was now looking straight at her, "when I saw you on that train in London and heard what you said, I couldn't believe my luck that this wonderful-looking girl was gazing straight at me and saying, even in jest, I was the sort of person you would like to marry. I knew I had to take that chance, do everything in my power to get to know you, even if it meant giving up my career in London and stepping into a venture which could have been very risky." So it was out at last. The question was answered. He had come deliberately. It was not an amazing coincidence.

"But my friend Flick…she had to come after you to give you my number."

"She didn't have far to go. I was already turning back to get on the train again before the doors closed, desperately afraid I wouldn't make it."

"Flick told me that you had my number."

"I tried. I did ring but you'd already gone. I think that was your English mobile. You have a different one here."

"Oh," she said, "yes, Flick told me you tried, but then how did you…?"

"You know your friend had taken my number too. She told me what had happened; that you had gone back to Italy because your father had died. She gave me your new number but I didn't think it was right to ring you in the circumstances if you had just lost your father. I thought I had lost you, that I had missed my chance." Gabriella was elated. It was all going to be alright. He was going to forgive her.

But then he said, "Flick told me someone was starting up a hotel and that you were involved. It seemed too good to be true. I was in the hotel business, I had already been thinking of coming back to Italy and getting away from city life. It seemed like fate, serendipity. I applied and you interviewed me. I thought you were the temporary manager. Your friend is a bit excitable. She may have told me it was yours but she was talking so fast I didn't take it in. Then it was only after you offered me the job I realised that you actually owned the place and that you were a Contessa. How could I have told you how I felt about you, about that instant attraction when we looked across that train carriage? People would think I was just after you for this place, for your title. My mother is from a peasant family in a smallholding near Assisi; my grandfather scraped a living; there was barely enough money to feed and clothe them, she and her sister. She met my father when she went as an au pair to England. She married him and stayed in England but they are still ordinary people living what you might call ordinary lives. They have nothing like this." He gestured with a wave of his hand around the Castello.

"But that is ridiculous," Gabriella burst out. "You know as well as I do how much I owe the bank. My father left me almost nothing. I had to beg the bank manager for an enormous overdraft to convert this place. It has become nothing but a burden, much as I love it. I could have sold it and gone back to being a student in London, made my own way in the world, but I felt it was my duty to keep it going for the sake of the people around me who were so loyal to my father for all those years. You said I treat people as if they were my servants. I am sorry once again if I gave you that impression but I would no more treat people here as if they were my servants than fly to the moon. Antonio, Carmela and Rosanna are like second parents to me. My mother died giving birth to me and, anyway," she threw in, "she was the daughter of one of the estate workers, not of so- called noble birth, and my father had to fight his father in order to marry her. Carmela and Rosanna have been like second mothers to me. Antonio was my father's friend and confidante, like a brother to him. If I had sold this place what would have happened to them? They might have been thrown on the scrap heap after all those years of devotion. If I hadn't cared about them and all those who work here, I wouldn't be fighting to keep this place going. As for the fact that I am a Contessa, that is rubbish. I am just Gabriella, fighting hard to keep everything and everyone I value in my life." She was nearly shouting at him. She paused to take a breath, willing him to react, to say something, anything, in return. For a long moment, he was silent.

Finally, he said, and his tone was more gentle, "Well, I did come back intending to give in my notice and move on but I understand what you say about making a go of things. I like living here and I like the challenge of making this place shine as it should." He paused again. He took a deep breath and finally made a decision. "Let us try and leave all the personal stuff out of it and concentrate on the job at hand, so I will stay if you still want me to."

"Yes please, Josh, please," she said simply.

"Ok then. Right, I will go upstairs and unpack but then when I come down, you can tell me what has been happening while I've been away." He didn't meet her eyes as he moved towards the stairs. She gave a huge sigh of relief that he was staying. As for his talk of 'personal stuff,' he had admitted that he was attracted to her, that he had come because of that ; that the attraction was strong enough for him to give up his job in England and take a chance on working in a place that was not even up and running. And in a way, she was grateful for Flick's excitable nature. If he had fully comprehended what she was saying, that the Castello was hers, he might have given up there and then and not come at all. So there was still hope and that would have to be enough for now.

Chapter 22

And in the meantime, as always, there was work to do. Easter was coming. There were Easter eggs for all the guests ready in their rooms. She still spent an hour at dawn each morning practising with Tosca, then it was back to change and get on with the business of the day. She was determined to be brisk and efficient and try and avoid being too much alone with Josh but it was difficult as they were in the office together constantly going over their plans. And she had plans, so many plans. She felt a thrill of excitement. It was so fulfilling, the challenge of providing a luxurious and interesting holiday for people. It was not a career she had ever dreamt of but it was surprisingly satisfying in every way. She realised what a wonderful path fate had taken her on, making people happy, giving them a comfortable room, good food and wine, keeping them entertained, showing off the beauty and wonderful landscape and interesting places of Tuscany. It had become the main focus of her life, her pride and joy.

Things slowly settled down between herself and Josh and soon, she felt the tension between them ebbing and they could talk normally again. Over Easter she took a party of English visitors firstly to Pienza to watch the Easter procession with twelve penitents walking barefoot and the statue of the Virgin being carried to the Duomo, a file of townspeople walking solemnly in line behind. Then they went on to San Gimignano 'the town of the towers'. It was one of Tuscany's marvels, encircled by thirteenth-century walls which she pointed out as Tommaso drove them towards it, the town sited high on a hill.

The skyline was filled with towering skyscrapers. They parked and walked through the medieval gate to the ancient triangular square dating back to Etruscan times. She explained that the town was part of the old pilgrim route to Rome where travellers stopped to refresh themselves. They stopped in a restaurant with a terrace looking out over a field of sunflowers, not in bloom yet but Gabriella explained that they were called 'Girasole' in Italian; literally 'turn towards the sun' which is exactly what they did, turn their heads to follow the sun as it moves around.

"Oh, we never noticed that," said several of the guests. "We just thought it was because they looked like the sun. That's cool!"

"And the towers, why the towers?" Someone else asked.

"Ah, we always joke that someone built a tower and the next person built a taller one to be better than his neighbour, then the next built an even taller one and so on."

"What you might call keeping up with the Joneses as we say in England." Someone else laughed.

"Exactly." Gabriella laughed. "There are seventy-two of them in all. You can climb one of them if you like."

"No thanks, I'm much too comfortable sitting her eating this lovely cake. What is it?"

"It's a panettone, which literally means 'big bread', the same as we eat at Christmas, but it's a special Easter one. Can you see it's in the shape of a dove?"

"Oh yes, so it is."

"You speak very good English," someone commented.

"I spent nearly three years in London, studying."

"Then why did you come back?" came the curious question.

Gabriella hesitated. She didn't want to have to explain about her father's death and the financial situation so she merely said, "I felt like a fresh challenge and this seemed like the right time."

"Well, you seem to be doing it well. That manager chap of yours is very efficient."

"I'm glad to hear it. I think he is."

"You need to hang on to him." If anyone noticed her blush, they didn't say anything.

"I intend to," she replied. The next morning, Easter Sunday, Carmela, ever inventive, had arranged decorated boiled eggs on the breakfast table. Added to this, they had a family, the first they had had staying, with two young children. Josh had arranged an Easter egg hunt in the area around the house and they stood together watching in amusement, together with the parents, as the children raced from tree to tree, flower pot to flower pot, screaming in excitement every time they found a chocolate egg. They raced up to Josh eventually, showing him their haul of eggs and watching him with the children she could see what a good father he was going to make one day. He sat with them on the terrace and they were enthralled, sitting wide-eyed as he told them stories about the Castello and its history, and when their parents told them it was time to leave as they had to go to lunch with friends there were wails of protest.

The next day, Easter Monday, she took the adult guests to another of her favourite places that was also on the route the pilgrims took. It was a tiny little hamlet high in the Tuscan hills where the village square was in fact filled with thermal water. It was called Bagno Vignoni and it was well known for its spa. "It's famous for being the Baths of Saint Catherine and has been visited by popes and many artists," she told them. They sat under the pines gazing out at the surrounding hills eating the picnic Lucia had prepared of salami, ham and cheese and fresh ripe tomatoes and apricots and drinking wine brought from the hotel.

"They call Easter Monday 'Pasquetta' in Italy," she explained. "Little Easter. A time for picnics and some fun after the solemnity of Easter itself." At that, she persuaded them to take off their shoes and socks and cool their feet in the little channel of thermal water that ran from the square. They all sat on the ground paddling in the rivulet of water, chatting amiably to each other.

"This is what I call a real holiday," said one of the guests. "Takes me back to my childhood when I used to paddle in the sea." She giggled and all the rest laughed and agreed it was the most beautiful and peaceful place they had ever been to.

"I can see why people come here on pilgrimage," someone said. "It's idyllic." It was a hard job to get them rounded up, shoes and socks on and back into the minibus for the trip back to the hotel. Gabriella had to dangle the thought of one of Carmela's excellent dinners in front of them to make them move; they were so comfortable, watching the sun slowly going down in splendour over the hills. In fact, the food was so good that evening that several of the guests asked for recipes, which Carmela was only too delighted to give them.

"I can see cookery classes coming as another sideline," Josh commented as they watched the guests clustered around the kitchen table, busily making notes.

"Exactly," Gabriella answered. "Maybe something for the quieter months."

"Quite." They beamed at each other and then both of them quickly looked away, afraid of seeming too intimate. Since they had admitted their feelings to each other, they had tried to keep them under wraps and deal just with day-to-day business. But an uneasy truce was taking place and Gabriella could only hope he would eventually forgive and forget her stupid mistake.

Chapter 23

That group departed, several of them vowing to return. The fame of the hotel was spreading so much that on Gabriella's next trip to Arezzo to discuss an order with one of her suppliers, she was infuriated to discover that he had been in conversation with Domenico. "Your cousin Domenico telling me that you are doing a good job managing his hotel for him," the man said.

"I beg your pardon," Gabriella spluttered. "His hotel! I think you must be under a misapprehension. Domenico has absolutely nothing to do with the Castello. It is mine and mine alone and I have an excellent manager. Please spread that message among your friends if you don't mind."

"Oh, I'm sorry," the supplier said, looking confused, "I must have misunderstood. I thought he said…" he stopped, embarrassed.

Gabriella was absolutely livid. However was she ever going to stop her wretched cousin and his mother from interfering in her business and trying to sponge off her? She arrived back at the Castello, still fuming.

"What's happened?" Josh asked, seeing the look on her face. She explained. "Don't take it too much to heart," he said, trying to reassure her. "He can only boast but he can't actually do anything. He is harmless." But Gabriella wasn't sure that he was.

****

In the meantime, every spare moment she had was spent on Tosca, practising. She had gone to the little shop just off the main Corso in Arezzo where the lances were carved. She had known the old man who carved the lances since she was a child and she chatted to him for a while, catching up with his family news. Trying to look casual she had lifted up one of the lances and held it in her hand, pointing it as if jokingly at a target. She felt the weight of it, trying to match it with the branches she had found on the estate.

Tosca had soon got used to the new routine and seemed almost eager to start, each time galloping furiously towards the target. Time after time, she missed, only rarely connecting and never hitting the centre. She grew dispirited. One morning though she hit the bull's eye. She was exultant. She raised her fist in the air in triumph, standing on her stirrups in victory. She wheeled Tosca around and there was Antonio standing looking at her in astonishment. "So that's what you've been doing all these mornings you've been sloping off?" He said as she slipped off the saddle and stood beside him.

"Do you think I'm mad?" Gabriella grinned.

"I think you are your father's daughter. As you know he won the Golden Lance five times. But they've never allowed a woman to ride."

"Is there actually anything in the rules to say I can't?" She asked.

"I don't think so," he shook his head. "I think it's just custom. Perhaps they think a woman couldn't hold the weight of the lance."

"I'd thought of that. Of course, I don't have a proper one but I've tested the weight of my branch against the real lance and I've discovered it's just a matter of balance," Gabriella said. "If you hold it in the right way, you don't feel the weight. No, the real test was getting Tosca accustomed to having a pole in her eyeline, but she's used to it now." She gazed at Antonio, then said earnestly, "I'd like to try. Do you think they would consider me?" He hesitated and then he said gravely. "Well, ordinarily, they would dismiss you out of hand, but seeing who you are, the daughter of a famous champion, I think they might be forced to consider you."

"I could always sue them under the sexual equality act," she laughed, "but seriously, Antonio, I'd like to try. You know the right people. It's not a case of nepotism. I know I have to be as good as or better than any man but I am happy to practice day and night to get it right."

"Gabriella, you are fantastic." Antonio laughed and hugged her. "I'm sure your father is looking down and smiling from ear to ear."

Chapter 24

Gabriella was in her bedroom searching on the Internet with her laptop. She had had the idea of watching her father's old triumphs at the joust. She could surely pick up a few hints of his technique by seeing how he prepared himself, how he began his run up the sand strip, the pace he rode at and the way he balanced the lance.

She went back a long way to the time of his first triumph four years before she was born. She fast-forwarded through swathes of pictures showing the gatherings in each quarter, the blessings in the churches, the processions through the city, the buglers signifying the start of the ceremony from the balcony of their own palazzo, the entrance into the square of the bands, the flag bears, the captains on their steady mounts with their entourages, the pikes, the crossbows, until she reached what she wanted: the moment her father, dressed in the red and green Santa Crucifera costume, could be seen entering on his stallion Itallo through the securely guarded gate at the bottom left-hand corner of the square.

There he was, wheeling Itallo around just inside the gate to steady him then slowly coming to a standstill, waiting as the lance was brought down to him: then leaning forward his eyes fixed on the target in a moment of supreme concentration, the halberd in line with his eyes. Itallo, unnerved again by the roar of the crowd, held by the groomsman to steady him, the camera panning round to show the nervous onlookers holding their breath. Then away he went, the lance lowered, the sound of the galloping horse, the bang as the point of the lance hit the target, the Burrata's metal chains swinging round, the screams of joy from the Porta Crucifera quarter as they realised it was a good score. Then he was out of sight around the top of the square, going so fast it took him a few moments to stop. And there too was a very young Antonio, helping him dismount, embracing him in joy.

Then the tense wait while the target was taken to the judges with their long red robes and white caps, the messenger taking the result to the Master of the Field. The dramatic pause.

Then finally the announcement that he had scored five points which meant his quarter had won; the ecstatic crowds bearing him on their shoulders triumphantly towards the cathedral to give thanks for their victory.

It was as if she had been there, her face alight with joy, sharing his triumph all over again.

Then she scrolled forward. She knew the years of his triumphs so she skipped the following year and started on the next year when he had won again. As she was fast-forwarding through the first part of the festivities, she saw the crowd gathering outside their own palazzo in the square. Then the camera panned up to show the crowd standing on their own balcony.

She was stunned. She saw herself leaning on the rail of the balcony. There was no mistaking herself, the same long black hair, the same vivid green eyes.

But how could that be? This was three years before she was born.

It was impossible. Had she entered some strange time warp?

As she was staring there was a knock on the door and a voice said, "Permesso? May I?"

"Come in," she called.

It was Rosanna, coming in to bring her fresh bed linen.

"Oh, Rosanna," she said. "It's you. Tell me who this is. I thought for a moment I was going mad and it was me standing in the balcony of the palazzo in the square, but this is a film of the joust three years before I was born."

Rosanna came round to look and sank onto the bed. "Madonna Gabriella, it's your mother!"

Gabriella was shocked into silence. Of course, it was. She had seen many photos of her mother and knew she looked like her but had never seen her moving, talking, or laughing with her friends. Tears sprang into her eyes.

"Oh, Rosanna, she's lovely. I never thought to see her as if she were alive. What is she saying? Can you make it out?"

They both stared, trying to lip-read.

Finally Rosanna said, "No, I can't. But it's enough that you've seen her. I'm so pleased for you."

They rewound the film several times and Gabriella knew that she would be able to do that time and time again to remember her mother's every gesture, every expression until they were ingrained in her mind forever and she could feel somehow close to a mother she had obviously been too young to recall, which was a comfort.

Finally, after a long time, she scrolled forward and they turned their attention to her father, watching him line up his lance, gallop to the target and once again be carried off in triumph.

She glanced up and Rosanna's eyes were glistening with tears. There was something about the rapt expression on her face, a look of complete adoration, that amazed Gabriella. Of course, Gabriella realised with a start. Why had she never understood? Rosanna had never married. She had been in love with Gabriella's father.

Poor Rosanna. She must be grieving as much as I am, Gabriella thought. But it was not her place to say anything. It was Rosanna's secret to carry to her grave. It would only embarrass her to talk about it.

Finally, she closed the laptop and vowed to watch the rest, his other three victories, another day.

And maybe, just maybe, with any luck, she would be able to see her mother again in one of the other films and feel even closer to her.

Chapter 25

She was on her way south to Assisi, over the border from Tuscany into Umbria. The road was straight and she was tempted to drive at her usual fast pace but she slowed deliberately to look around her at the magnificent scenery, considered by most people to be the most beautiful in all of Italy with its rolling green hills, wide forests, tumbling rivers and lush farmland, vineyards and fields of sunflowers. Nearby were the wonderful towns, villages and cities of Perugia, Orvieto, Montalcino, Gubbio, Cortona and Pienza but of all the hill towns in Italy Assisi was one of the most spectacular because of its art, architecture and history. It was the birthplace of Saint Francis, patron saint of animals who was a soldier until his conversion to God and who was so beloved that they say 3,000,000 people attended his funeral. She loved the idea of the humble little church he started with, later built over several times so that the present-day church consisted of the upper church, the lower church and the crypt, the upper church decorated with wonderful frescoes and paintings by the artist Giotto.

She parked and slipped into the church to admire the frescoes once again and to light a candle for her parents. Then it was time for work. She went to the travel agent in the main square to meet her friend Monica who had founded the now flourishing business some four years before. She and Monica hugged. They hadn't seen each other in over three years but had been best friends at school. She had been one of the first people Gabriella talked to on the phone when she had decided to open the Castello as a hotel and Monica had been incredibly encouraging and supportive in helping her, by promoting the hotel to everyone enquiring about luxury hotels in the region.

After she had filled Monica in on the progress of the business and the new facilities and trips they were planning in order to update the agency website, Monica left one of her colleagues in charge and they went for a coffee and a private catch-up. Monica had a steady boyfriend, someone they both knew from school days and it seemed likely they would marry soon. "And you?"

Monica asked. Gabriella was silent, but she could feel the blush spreading slowly up over her cheeks. "Ah," Monica said, "so there is someone you are interested in."

"You won't actually what I am about to tell you," Gabriella said. She started the familiar story with the day on the tube and how her English friend Flick had chased him to get his number and how he was actually turning back to get her number: how subsequently he had applied for the job to be her manager and everything that had happened since. She was right, Monica couldn't quite believe what she was hearing. She sat open-mouthed in astonishment.

"So let me get this right. It was love at first sight on a train and then he threw up his job in London to come to Italy. It sounds like a match made in heaven to me. So what exactly is the problem? Or am I missing something here?"

"The problem," said Gabriella slowly, trying to suppress the tears welling up in her eyes, "is that once he discovered I was a Contessa and owned the Castello, he has got this stupid idea that he is not worthy of me, however much I tell him that being a Contessa these days in Italy doesn't mean a thing."

"But he's still around so that must mean something."

"Yes," agreed Gabriella. "I pray that someday he'll change his mind." She paused. "I wanted to ask you. I know he possibly didn't come to Italy just for me. What I didn't tell you is that his mother is Italian."

"It gets even better," grinned Monica, "he is half-Italian."

"But his mother lives in England, married to an Englishman. Her sister though, runs an agriturismo somewhere near here. I know he came to stay there recently and I wondered if you had any ideas."

"Well, I know several in the area but there is one which is highly recommended with a lot of repeat customers. Like all the others, it used to be a working farm until it opened up to receive guests. They do bed and breakfast and the occasional evening meal to order. I could make some discrete enquiries about their relatives in England or we could drive out there and see them."

"I'd love to but Josh would think I was snooping. I'd hate to go behind his back."

"Josh? Joshua?" Monica frowned. "Giosue in Italian? My brother knew a boy who came to Italy on holiday to stay with his aunt. I will ask him and let you know." They parted at last, vowing to meet up again before too long. "In Bocca al Lupo," they hugged. "In the mouth of the wolf," the usual Italian blessing for good luck.

"Before I go," Gabriella said, "where is the agriturismo you mentioned? The best one?" Monica gave her directions; they hugged again and Gabriella sped away. She knew the road and the area well. The old farmhouse was perched high on a hill outside the town. She lingered outside, gazing at the vineyard with its just burgeoning leaves, the very beginning of fruit appearing. Beyond that, she could see olive trees and rows of farm buildings obviously converted into accommodation for travellers who wanted somewhere to stay with the real flavour of the region. Hence the name agriturismo, a corruption of agricultural tourism, which had become so popular in recent years. They were cheaper than a hotel but also a chance to stay on a working farm, sample wine, olive oil and fresh produce straight from the farm as well as mingling with real Italians in beautiful countryside. There was a lot to be said for it.

Beyond the rooms, she could just make out a swimming pool where a few people sat on loungers watching children splash in the pool. She could see no sign of anyone who looked as if they worked there and, as she had said to Monica, she dared not go nearer in case it was the right place and Josh thought she was snooping. If this business belonged to his aunt she could see how he felt it couldn't compare to the luxury of the Castello with its grandeur and noble lineage. "What was it that made one person superior to another in social circles?" She asked herself. They often got where they were by sheer brutality or sheer wealth, nothing to do with their good character or how well they treated their fellow human beings.

She sighed, took a deep breath and drove home feeling slightly depressed.

Chapter 26

They had a difficult customer. So far, most of their guests had been delightful, appreciative of the comfortable rooms, the excellent food that Carmela produced and the wonderful grounds in which to walk and admire the views of the wooded slopes of the Apennines.

But no, that wasn't enough for one single man who complained from the moment he arrived that the water in his bathroom wasn't the right temperature, the food was too rich (Gabriella had trouble stopping Carmela hitting him with a rolling pin), that the bed was too soft and that he had got mud on his designer shoes walking in the garden. "Well, he'd better watch where he puts his feet," Josh muttered under his breath, before turning to smile politely at the next guest.

In fact, he had upset Gabriella from the start by walking past her as she stood to greet him in the doorway the morning he mounted the steps, ignoring her completely.

She moved after him asking if she could help but he walked towards Josh and said brusquely, "Ah, you must be the owner. I hope I am going to get really good service here and not be palmed off with one of your lesser employees," an obvious allusion to her.

William politely tried to explain that he wasn't the owner and pointed out that he had actually just passed Gabriella in the doorway, who was, but the man barely glanced at her as if a mere girl was unable to fulfil his demands which turned out to be loud and frequent The trouble was, as Gabriella had rapidly learned, the unpleasant guests upset the atmosphere for the others. She and Josh both tried to steer him away from everyone else when he started to complain but his voice was so strident it was difficult to get him out of earshot. "I think I know what his game is," Josh said. "If he had a genuine complaint, that would be different but I think he's hoping that if he complains enough we will reduce his bill or even cancel it altogether."

Gabriella admired Josh's skill at dealing with the obnoxious man who finished every scrap of his meal before telling Josh that he hadn't enjoyed it. He indicated loudly that he wouldn't be recommending that his friends stay at the Castello and that he had some very influential friends. Gabriella was tempted to say that she was delighted to hear that he wouldn't be back, but Josh flashed her a warning look. The man departed at last, having, as Josh suspected, negotiated a reduction in his bill which they had reluctantly agreed to just to get rid of him. "I've started a blacklist," Josh said as they watched his car drive away. "He's on top of it."

"No, second," said Gabriella. "Don't forget Domenico."

"Ah yes," Josh said ruefully. Then Rosanna came downstairs in a state of great agitation. It took them a few moments to understand what she was so indignant about. It turned out that he had purloined a rather beautiful bowl from his room, together with the bathrobe and several towels.

"Wicked, wicked man," Rosanna was almost crying. She was taking the theft personally, almost as if she had been responsible for the loss and it took Gabriella a while to calm her down.

"After we take such care to make the rooms look beautiful," she wailed. "How can people be so bad?"

Finally, after a cup of strong coffee and one of Carmela's excellent cakes, she was calm enough to resume her duties upstairs. To vent her frustration Gabriella excused herself and spent an hour in the stables, mucking them out and grooming Tosca which always calmed her down. Josh had followed her and stood watching, leaning against the door jamb, as she picked up the curry comb and brushed Tosca's flanks with rhythmic strokes. "You really love that horse," he smiled.

"She was a present from my father for my eighteenth birthday," Gabriella said. "I really missed her when I was in London."

"I'm sure you did and I'm sure she missed you."

Gabriella smiled at him.

"I think she did." Then she burst out. "That awful man. How could you bear to be so polite to him?"

"You get used to it," he shrugged. "There's always one who is impossible to please. Of course, things do go wrong, it's inevitable and if it's a genuine problem, we can try and fix it but there are a few people like him who try to get away with as much as they can."

"And to add insult to injury, stealing things as well."

"That's nothing," he grimaced. "Some people think that if they are paying for a room, they are entitled to take what they like, especially if a company is footing the bill and it is difficult to challenge them. I've known furniture go down the fire escape into a van and people in big hotels walking out boldly with valuable items past the staff. If they look assured enough, the staff assume they are taking something to be repaired. Then there was the woman who booked into several hotels with large suitcases saying that her husband was coming later. She stripped the room of everything that could be moved, bedding, curtains, even rugs and loaded them in the car during the night."

"So did they catch her in the end?"

"Yes, because hotels have connections with each other and the managers circulated her description. One manager recognised her and phoned the police. They had to wait until she had the stuff actually in the car before they swooped. We did have one amusing theft though," he went on. "If you can call any theft amusing. One of the hotels reported two valuable plates missing that had been on stands in a bedroom. The receptionist remembered that the couple had booked a night in another hotel in the next county so they rang and asked if they could discreetly search the couple's luggage, which the staff duly did while the pair were having dinner. The plates were found and eventually returned to the first hotel and of course, the couple in question had no way of complaining."

"Result!" laughed Gabriella. "I had no idea it was that bad. I'm glad we've locked all the valuables away though I suppose someone could still get at them if they were determined."

"I am afraid it happens. We got away lightly. In fact."

"My father would have just thrown him out on his ear."

"But then your father wasn't in the hotel business. Getting angry or rude doesn't help. And we always run the danger of getting sued if we accuse someone wrongly."

"No," she replied, realising she had just reminded him of the fact that her father had been all-powerful, that he was the ruler of his entire domain and his word was law.

In other words, an aristocrat. She tried to change the subject. " Do you think you could hold Tosca's head for a moment while I check her hooves?"

"Of course," he moved to take the halter and in doing so had to brush past her. They stood for a moment close together and she held her breath, longing for him to reach out and hold her close. Then she heard him take a swift intake of breath as he slid past her to take hold of the halter and the moment had gone. She busied herself with lifting each of Tosca's hooves to examine them for problems but she could hardly concentrate with him standing nearby. When she looked up, he was stroking Tosca's mane in fierce concentration as if afraid that looking at her would ignite the flame. "Ready?" He said finally.

"Yes, thank you."

"Then I must get back to work." And he walked back past her without meeting her eyes and she gazed after him as he crossed the yard, with a feeling that was becoming all too familiar to her, a longing to throw herself into his arms and the equally strong knowledge that he would resist her and she would feel a fool.

Chapter 27

Things continued well for a while at the hotel, much to Gabriella's relief, with satisfied guests and trips guided by her to the wine villages of Montepulciano and Montalcino where she had arranged lectures in the wine cellars on the rich red wines the region produced, especially the world-famous Brunello de Montalcino. The minibus was often clanking with bottles as Tommaso drove home as most of the guests took advantage of buying wine straight from the vineyards. She led art tours on the trail of Piero Della Francesca, both in Arezzo at the Duomo with its portrait of Mary Magdalene and the church of San Francesco with the fresco cycle of the Legend of the True Cross as well as in the surrounding villages. In Monterchi, they marvelled at the only fresco in existence of the pregnant Madonna, her hand resting serenely on her bump while teenage angels flanked her holding back the canopy. In his home town of San Sepulchro, she showed them the fresco of the Resurrection of Christ with Christ triumphantly holding aloft his flag while soldiers slept at his feet. Then there was a day at Monteriggioni, a wonderful walled medieval town where the castle walls offered spectacular views of the Tuscan countryside.

She kept busy and out of Josh's way most of the time as he continued to run things efficiently and smoothly. There were always a few ups and downs of course. She filled in one day as she often did when Rosanna had a doctor's appointment or one of the girls who helped out was off and they had had a guest who left the room in a complete mess. She could never quite believe how some people treated hotel rooms. "They would never do this at home," she said, as she cleared empty wine bottles from under the sideboard and rehung the curtains. "What on earth were they doing here? Playing Tarzan?" She said as she stood on a stepladder trying to hook the curtains back onto the rail.

"I've seen worse," the girl shrugged. "Some people leave the room as tidy as they can, even cleaning the bath and sink. Others seem to think they are paying for the room so we are here to clear up their mess. Heaven knows what their houses are like."

Then one day they had a world-famous guest.

Lucia squealed in excitement when Gabriella announced his name to the staff.

His face had rarely been off the TV screen for the past twenty years and he had made countless well-known films and won several Oscars.

His agent had rung to make the booking, stressing that the name of the Castello had come up as being a small exclusive place where his client could rest and recuperate after a stressful year of filming during which his father, to whom he had been very close, had died and he, the actor, had been unwell. He required as much privacy as possible for someone so famous, so he hoped the staff would oblige and try to keep any curious clients from bothering him as much as possible.

Josh communicated all of this to the staff.

"Strictly no autographs or selfies," he instructed. "Just treat him the way you would any other customer, with courtesy. I think he may keep to his room a lot but if he does come down we need to try and avoid any of the other guests bothering him by distracting them politely. It will be inevitable I suppose that some of them will, but that can't be helped. We must all do our best."

A chauffeur-driven car drew up on the appointed day and the star got out, the man who was obviously his agent helping him with his luggage which Tommaso moved to take charge of immediately.

Josh showed him up to his room but Gabriella couldn't help noting as he passed her how tired and drawn he looked and thought how grief and strain were no respecters of persons, however famous.

For the first few days, he stayed in his room, just calling down for meals when he needed them which Josh took to him personally.

On the fourth morning, Gabriella, as was her wont, rose early to go and practise with Tosca and almost bumped into a figure in the garden as she walked through on her way to the stables. It was the actor, obviously thinking no one was about at that hour of the morning.

"Oh, I'm sorry. I didn't mean to disturb you," she said.

"No, I'm sorry," he replied. He already looked better. He had obviously slept a lot and Rosanna had made sure he had some extra pillows and anything else he required. "This is a lovely place," he continued. "Is it yours? I think they told me some young Contessa owned it."

"Yes, it's my family home," Gabriella replied. "It has only become a hotel fairly recently."

"Well, you've done a good job of it. Your food is delicious. Your chef is very good. Not fancy, just very wholesome and I think probably typically Tuscan."

"Yes, our chef is a woman, Carmela. I can introduce you if you like and if you ask her for any special dishes I am sure she would be delighted to make them for you."

"And I would be delighted to meet her." He smiled and her heart fluttered. She could see how his charm and talent as an actor had won so many admirers.

Then she said regretfully, "I must go. I have an appointment with a horse." She smiled at him.

"Yes, I've watched you from the window. You are quite the rider."

"Thank you." Then she added, "Would you like to meet her?"

"I'd be delighted."

She led him through the garden to the stables and he spent some time stroking and admiring Tosca. At one point, she could see his face working with emotion and he finally said, "My father loved horses. He was also a rider."

"You must miss him very much."

"I do. He was always so supportive of me following my dream and becoming an actor when most parents would have been horrified at their child following such a precarious profession."

"Well, you certainly must have made him very proud with the all things you have achieved."

"I hope I did."

There was a pause and then he said, "I'm holding you up, you must get your ride."

Gabriella swung into the saddle and as she urged Tosca out of the stable, he called after her, "Don't forget to introduce me to your cook."

"I won't," Gabriella called back before she urged Tosca into a trot and then a canter.

That evening instead of staying in his room, he came down to dinner with the other guests. Josh put him on a table on the terrace facing out over the view, so he had his back to the other guests and didn't have to endure the inevitable stares and whispers.

"Fame has its price," she whispered to Josh and he nodded in agreement.

Then after dinner, she led him into the kitchen where Lucia nearly dropped the saucepan she was cleaning. Carmela, flushed pink with excitement, took his proffered hand and Gabriella wondered if she would refrain from washing it for the next week.

He said some very kind words about her cooking and then left to go up to his room but the following morning when she went at eleven to have a quick coffee in the kitchen she found him sitting there watching Carmela and Lucia working.

"I hope you don't mind. I don't want to hold them up but it's so soothing watching them preparing the food, making pasta and cakes and stirring the sauces. I promise not to get in the way."

And so it was that gradually, after dinner, it became a ritual that he would go and sit in the kitchen where Gabriella, Josh, Carmela, Lucia, Antonio and Rosanna would gather and he would tell them stories of the films he had made and occasionally, as he regained his strength, telling them scurrilous pieces of gossip about some famous film stars while Gabriella and Josh in turn translated for the open-mouthed staff.

On a couple of days, Gabriella drove him around some of the local famous villages and then took him into Arezzo where he admired the square, the fort and the various churches. She was amused when more than once people looked, then did a double take, nudged their neighbours and stared but she moved him swiftly on before he could be pestered, although he did stop for a couple of selfies and autographs with good grace, smiling at her ruefully before surrendering to the inevitable group of hysterical fans.

On the way home, wincing at the speed she drove at, he said, while clutching at the dashboard, "You're a very beautiful lady and forgive me if I speak out of turn but I'd have made a pass at you if I hadn't felt your affections were directed elsewhere. Am I correct?"

Gabriella was stunned into silence and for a moment nearly lost control of the car. One of the most famous stars in the world was talking about making a pass at her but it was also the fact that he'd realised her feelings for Josh. Were they that obvious to everyone?

"Have I upset you?" He said.

"No," she replied. "You are right, and thank you for the compliment."

"I meant it."

Then he continued, "And I may as well continue putting my foot in it and tell me if it's none of my business but I think he feels the same way so what's the problem?"

"It's, it's," she hesitated.

"The Castello…and the fact you are a Contessa?" He suggested. "He doesn't feel worthy of you."

She slowed right down and then looked at him.

"You are very shrewd," she smiled. "Exactly that."

"Well, I must say he's a very foolish man. If I had been in his position, I wouldn't have hesitated for a second."

"Good of you to say so."

"No really. I hope he sees sense in the end."

"So do I…perhaps a real Hollywood ending where the music rises to a crescendo and the pair of us walk into the sunset holding hands you mean." She was grinning at him, her mouth twisted into a wry smile. "You would know all about that."

"Exactly." He grinned back as they stopped in front of the Castello. They both saw Josh watching them arrive from his viewpoint in the lounge.

The famous actor grinned at her again. "Let's make him jealous," he said.

He leaned over and kissed Gabriella.

And, after a moment's hesitation, she kissed him right back.

****

He stayed a month and at the end of it, he went round hugging all the staff in turn, saving a special hug for Carmela who had frequently made him some of the special dishes he had requested.

"I will never forget you all," he said. "You have saved my sanity. It has been one of the best months of my life. I will recommend you to all my friends."

Again Lucia squealed in excitement at the thought of more famous actors and actresses coming to stay.

They stood outside in a line as he finally departed, not before a last lingering look at Gabriella and a rueful smile. His agent who had come to collect him, also thanked them for making him so comfortable and restoring him to health again. As he waved from his chauffeur-driven car, Gabriella couldn't resist a sideways glance at Josh who, as usual, was looking inscrutable. Did she detect though a frisson of relief that the actor had gone, or was it only wishful thinking?

"Well," said Carmela. "The next time I go to the cinema, no one seeing him on the screen will believe that he actually sat in my kitchen and even gave me a hug."

"Well, he's just a man after all, not a god, but I'm glad we were able to make him feel so much at home," said Gabriella and Josh, not quite meeting her gaze, nodded in approval and added, "Well done, everyone. And now," he added firmly, "it's back to work."

Chapter 28

On the day after he left, Josh slipped as he was coming down the stairs, and in reaching for the banister to stop himself from falling, he sprained his wrist. Wincing with pain, he staggered into the kitchen. He sat for a moment, trying to recover himself with Carmela, all concern, taking his arm to see how much damage there was. Gabriella, coming into the kitchen at that precise moment, could see him sitting white-faced at the table. "What is it?" She asked in alarm. Carmela looked up.

"It's not broken," she said. She turned her attention to Josh. "It's a bad sprain though. You'll have to be careful for the next week or so." He nodded, unable to speak. Gabriella went upstairs and brought down one of her scarves and some painkillers; Carmela fashioned an old-fashioned sling with the scarf, then gave him a glass of water and a strong coffee. After a while, he had recovered himself and tried to get up. "Sorry," he said. "To be a nuisance."

"For heaven's sake," Carmela and Gabriella said simultaneously. "You couldn't help it." So he carried on, able to do most of the tasks in the hotel except carrying things. Then one morning, a few days later, he came hurrying to Gabriella with a problem. "I've just had a call from my uncle," he said with a worried expression, "I need to get there. They think my aunt may have had a stroke and I don't know how bad it is. The trouble is I can't drive with this arm out of action. Do you think Tommaso could take me?"

"Tommaso has just gone to the city to pick up a delivery," Gabriella said. She thought swiftly. "Give me ten minutes to arrange cover here and I'll take you." He was about to protest but she had already gone into the kitchen to speak to Carmela and ask her to talk to Gianetta and Marco, the young people they had employed, who seemed bright enough and who could attend to any of the guests' needs. "We should be back for the evening service. If things are serious, I can leave Josh there and go back for him later."

They drove in silence along the autostrada with Josh sitting tensely beside her and after just over an hour, he said, "Turn off here." Her guess had been right. It was the agriturismo she had seen from the road, the one Monica had said was the best in the area. She was excited to see it. It would be interesting to discover more about Josh's family. As they drove towards the farmhouse, they could see a man running out of the main door. She skidded to a halt and Josh was out of the car and rushing to meet him. They embraced, then walked together to the house, deep in conversation. Gabriella, afraid of intruding, remained in the car for a few minutes, then decided to get out and walk around a little. She admired the neat vegetable patch and the small beehive which was buzzing with activity and was just thinking of walking towards the vineyard when she saw them coming out towards her.

" I'm so sorry, Gabriella, I didn't think, I was so anxious to find out what was happening," Josh said.

"Don't worry, I quite understand," Gabriella assured him. "How is she?"

"Not nearly as bad as we thought. The doctor has been and in fact, it was a false alarm, thank heavens. The doctor thinks it was a dizzy turn brought on by a virus and too much sun. Oh and this is my uncle Renato." Gabriella shook hands with him and gazed at the kindly face, grizzled with stubble and weatherbeaten by wind, rain and sun from working in the fields.

"I am sorry about your wife," she said.

"Thank you," he replied. Then he added, "Come, you must be thirsty after your drive." They went into the homely kitchen, old-fashioned and comfortable with an ancient dresser full of mismatched china, a scrubbed wooden table and a cat which rose to meet her and wove its way round her legs hoping for milk. They sat and drank at the table and Renato produced a tin of biscuits. "My wife made these," he offered one to Gabriella.

"They are excellent. Please tell her."

"You can tell her yourself. She is in bed but she is anxious to meet you." They went from the kitchen along a corridor to a simple bedroom. The light was dim but Gabriella could make out a figure propped up in bed bolstered by a pile of pillows. "Zia Paola, this is Gabriella, my boss, who drove me here." His aunt struggled to raise herself on her pillows. She looked very pale. Gabriella couldn't help but think of the stroke her father had had, which had resulted in his death. Thank heavens this in fact had not been the same. All she needed, it seemed, was a period of rest and care.

"Piacere, pleased to meet you." Gabriella gazed down at the figure in the bed. Even in her enfeebled state, Gabriella could see the family likeness. They were a handsome clan.

"Ah, the Contessa. Josh has told us so much about you. In fact, he can speak of little else. I am glad to see that you are in fact quite normal, not like a royal figure at all. I was expecting a crown at least."

"Zia!" Josh said, acutely embarrassed. His uncle Renato laughed.

"You can see my wife is not that ill after all. She is accustomed to speaking her mind." Gabriella laughed.

"I've left the crown at home. I only wear it when I go to meet the King of England on royal occasions." They spent a few more minutes at her bedside, then they could see she was getting tired.

"Come," her husband said, "I will show you around. It is very simple, not like I imagine your Castello to be." And it was indeed very simple, but all the better for it. In fact, it was totally delightful. The rooms with wooden beams above were whitewashed and there were bright hangings on the walls, quilted bedcovers and painted shutters, knotted rugs on the colourful tiled floors, pictures of farm animals on other walls.

"My aunt painted these," Josh said proudly.

"They are very good. She is talented."

"She wanted to go to art college when she was young but there wasn't the money for it and then she married my uncle and became a farmer's wife."

"She expresses her talent in the way she has decorated these rooms," Gabriella said. "They're charming."

"I will tell her you said so," Josh smiled gratefully. They had got used to speaking in a mixture of Italian and English but now they spoke in Italian because of his uncle. He seemed more relaxed now that he knew his aunt was alright, in fact, more relaxed than she had ever seen him. He was on his own territory she thought and he felt at home. They went outside. The pool looked inviting. In fact, it was a better pool than the one they had at the Castello. Gabriella made a mental note that one day they would build a new one. They wandered further afield. The views were magnificent, a valley full of olive trees, fields of sun flowers now fully out.

"Complimenti," she said. "It is all lovely. I could happily spend a week here. I am sure your guests have a wonderful time."

"It was my aunt's idea to open it up to visitors," Josh said. "You can see she is the driving force in the family." He laughed. "It was difficult to keep afloat with just the farm, as with many others, so she was among the first to have the idea of converting the old farm buildings into bedrooms. She's also a great cook so she does the catering as well. I admire her enormously. She is a real Wonder Woman, brave and fearless, just like you," he added, then he flushed.

"Thank you," Gabriella blushed too and they walked in an awkward silence for a moment. Then Gabriella said, "Well, she has obviously done an excellent job of it. But then I suppose some of the ideas came from you."

"Not at all. I think it's been the other way round in fact. She would have made an excellent hotel manager. Her attention to detail is amazing and her ideas keep coming. As her next project, she wants to keep sheep and milk them for pecorino cheese."

"Wow, that must be time-consuming. I've never seen sheep being milked, only goats."

"Oh, she'll probably go on to goat's cheese as well," he laughed. They looked at the little vineyard from which his uncle made his own wine and there was a yard full of clucking hens and an important-looking rooster who made his presence felt loudly and noisily every five minutes. There were the inevitable cats slinking around the barn and a dog, a black Labrador who nuzzled her in search of treats.

"This is paradise, Josh," she said and he looked suitably pleased. "I must leave you and go and do some work," his uncle said. "There is more to do than ever now Paola is not well."

"I wish we could help," Gabriella said, "but we have to get back soon." They strolled down into the valley through the olive grove and then through a wild flower meadow brilliant with poppies. Josh stumbled and because his arm was in a sling, Gabriella automatically put out her hand to save him from falling. Her hand gripped his and she kept it firmly there. He didn't protest. It seemed to her that if she was going to convince him that they would have any sort of a future together, it was she who had to do all the running. Here they were on neutral ground, not in the Castello where he felt unworthy of her. So she continued to hold his hand as they walked and it felt comfortable and easy and when she leaned forward and kissed him gently on the mouth, for once he made no attempt to draw back. They stood together on the edge of a field of glorious sunflowers it all seemed so natural and perfect and she could only feel utter contentment.

They made their farewells and drove back, again in silence, but this time, it was a companionable silence, not wanting the spell of that beautiful place to be broken. Sadly, the spell was broken only too abruptly.

Chapter 29

As they drew up in front of the Castello, Gianetta, one of the young people left in charge, came rushing out. "I'm so glad you are here. Come, come quickly." Gabriella's heart sank. It was Domenico, quite obviously very drunk, sprawled on a chair on the terrace, declaring to the few guests who were there, that this was his inheritance and that she, Gabriella, had usurped his place, taking what was rightfully his. Even Cara, his mother, sitting next to him, had the grace to look ashamed at the disturbance. Josh immediately sprang into action. Despite his sprained wrist, he took hold of Domenico's arm with his other hand, and ignoring his loud protests, wheeled him smartly round to the side of the house. Cara followed meekly. Luckily, she was driving and he deposited Domenico in the back seat of the car. His protests eventually dwindled away and soon he lay down and began to snore loudly.

"If I see you here again, either of you," he said firmly to Cara, "I will call the police."

"You wouldn't dare," she quavered.

"Oh yes, I would," Josh reiterated. "You be sure of it." He helped her into the driving seat, closed the door firmly and he and Gabriella watched as she drove away, the car disappearing eventually round the curve of the drive.

"Thank you," Gabriella said.

"All part of the service," he smiled. She held his gaze. Something had shifted between them that day. The kiss between them had broken a barrier. Nothing had been said but the acknowledgement that there was more than a professional relationship gave her hope. She knew she must be patient and bide her time and hope that the seed that had been planted would flourish. She must give him space and not force the issue. But it was hard, so hard, when all she wanted was for him to take her in his arms and hold her close. They went back to the terrace and apologised to the guests for the disruption. Luckily, most of them didn't understand Italian and hadn't understood what he had been saying which was a relief as she didn't want rumours of family rifts to circulate. She offered them all a complimentary glass of Prosecco which of course they accepted with alacrity. "Your young man dealt with the matter very well," one of them commented. She didn't correct him about Josh being her young man. It had been a wonderful day and she dreamt that night of fields of sunflowers and felt the soft touch of his lips on hers.

Chapter 30

They were all gathered around the big table in the kitchen; Gabriella, Josh, Carmela and Antonio, Rosanna, Tommaso, Marco, Gianetta and Lucia. It was the 13th of June, Antonio's Onomastico, St Anthony's Day, the saint after whom he was named, and they were celebrating.

The guests had all gone out for the day so there was peace and quiet until dinner time and they were taking an hour off work for coffee and cake, a special Cassata cake that Carmela had made for Antonio because it was his favourite. She didn't allow him to have it very often, however much he begged because it was very rich and she was afraid for his arteries, consisting as it did of sponge cake soaked in orange liqueur, ricotta cheese, candied fruit and chocolate pieces. His eyes had lit up when he saw it and he planted a smacking kiss on her cheek. She beamed with pleasure.

Gabriella thought how lucky Italians were with their Saint's Day to celebrate as well as their birthdays. Sometimes their Saint's Day felt even more important. Normally, they would have had some Prosecco but of course, they all had to get back to work so coffee had to suffice.

Gabriella looked around her in satisfaction at her little family because that was what they felt like. Antonio was flushed with pleasure at all the attention he was getting. Carmela too was happy to have made him his favourite cake and brimmed with pride when they all pronounced it delicious and everyone had a second helping. Marco and Gianetta had proved to be stalwarts too, happy to turn their hands to anything asked of them, both cheerful and smiling with the guests and quietly efficient. Marco spoke German quite well as he had spent a year in Germany and he knew some English from school. Gianetta had spent a year in England and had a French mother so spoke well in both languages. Most guests, Gabriella had found, spoke English and that had proved to be the common language for those not speaking Italian. She herself had learned French at school so could converse in three languages.

Josh, having spent time at University in Switzerland, could speak four. Carmela and Antonio hadn't progressed much beyond 'Good morning' and 'Good evening' but Tommaso, who dealt with the guests' luggage and other requests had progressed quite well in some of the basic phrases in each language. They all had the odd problem when a guest spoke none of the above but luckily on those days, Google Translate was a godsend.

Now they toasted Antonio in coffee, polished off the cake and sat back replete. "I don't think I could eat again for a week," Lucia remarked with a sigh.

"Me neither," said Gabriella. "Carmela, you really are a marvel. We must get those cookery classes up and running."

"I'd love to," Carmela enthused.

Antonio cleared his throat and said, "If I may, I'd like to say a few words."

They all looked at him expectantly.

He looked directly at Gabriella.

"I really thought that when the old count died, Gabriella, you would sell up and that Carmela, myself and you Rosanna and Tommaso would be not only out of a job but also homeless as well. We were all fearful for our futures." He paused, then he continued, his voice full of emotion, "I cannot say how much I appreciate the fact that you have done your utmost to preserve the Castello and keep us all in employment. May God bless you Gabriella for your spirit and your determination and on behalf of us all, thank you."

There was silence for a moment and everyone wiped a tear from their eyes. They were all looking at her.

She swallowed. "Thank you, Antonio. I was determined not to let my father down and we seem to be making a success of this venture. I would never have willingly abandoned you all. But," she added, "I have to say our success is also due to you all and especially to Josh here," she looked directly at him and smiled, "for his skill and hard work. Without you, I wouldn't have known what to do."

Josh smiled back at her and said, "Thank you, Gabriella, and may I say it has been a pleasure working with you all."

Antonio added, "And, Josh, may I say you have helped me enormously with my accounts and I consider you a true friend and," he paused, emotion welling up again, "Carmela and I both agree you are like the son we never had."

Carmela nodded enthusiastically in agreement and Josh looked awkward but pleased at the same time.

There was another silence only broken eventually by Gabriella who said, "Thank you so much, Antonio, for all those kind words."

She paused and continued, in an effort to get everyone back on an even keel after all the emotions that had been aroused, "Now before we all start drowning in our own happy tears, perhaps it is time we all got on with our work. Especially as there is no more cake."

And they all laughed. And went back to work.

Chapter 31

Carmela was giving her first cookery lesson to a small group of guests. Nearly everyone who stayed had commented on her ice cream and how much better it was than anything they had ever eaten before. They all asked what it was that was different from ordinary ice cream, so Gabriella, who was translating for Carmela explained that gelato, although it was the Italian word for ice cream, was in fact made in a different way to the ice cream they were used to.

"Ice cream as the name suggests," she explained, "has more cream than milk and is frozen. Gelato is the other way around. It has more milk than cream and is never frozen solid. Also, ice cream has a minimum of ten per cent fat whereas gelato has only about five per cent fat."

" Goody," someone piped up, "so I can have more of it then!"

Everyone laughed. "But why does it taste better then, if it has less fat?"

"I'll explain. It's all to do with the way it's made. It was invented by the Romans but it was only in the Renaissance that the gelato we eat was refined."

As she paused and they all watched Carmela adding the ingredients, her mind drifted back to the previous week when she and Josh were in Arezzo again having just been to the travel agents. They had been sidetracked to the gelateria where, as always in Italy, there was a huge queue. They waited patiently in line chatting about business until it was their turn at the counter. They had stood, trying to decide which flavour out of the myriad on offer they would choose. Eventually, Gabriella opted for a mix of lemon and frutta do Bosco, a mix of berries, while Josh had chocolate and pistachio. Then there was a further decision to make, cup or cornet and if cornet, which size?

"So much hard work." Gabriella had laughed.

Finally, cornets in hand, they had emerged onto the street again laughing.

"Look out!" Josh had warned. "It's dripping."

He had reached over and run his hand down her arm with his hand to remove the gelato and she had felt something akin to an electric shock. Every fibre of her being had been alive to his touch.

"Thanks," she had murmured, trying to recover herself.

If he had noticed her reaction, he didn't say anything and they had walked in silence for a while eating their cornets.

How long can this go on for? Gabriella thought. *It's agony. I know he cares but why, oh why, is he so stubborn? How long can he resist?*

She was suddenly aware that Carmela was looking at her quizzically, waiting for her to translate and she had to wrench her mind back to the present.

"As you can see gelato is churned at a slower speed."

They all watched hypnotised as the mixture was churned.

"So now we can eat it?" A hopeful guest said.

"Sadly no. You'll have to wait for dinner. It will be frozen but not to the same temperature as ice cream. Gelato is served at a warmer temperature than ice cream so the mixture is silkier and softer. That's why it tastes better than ice cream because frozen food dulls the taste buds whereas the flavour comes through more with the gelato."

"I'm not sure I can wait until dinner," a guest muttered.

"Well, perhaps we can try it in a couple of hours. Special treat. In the meantime, Carmela is going to show you the right way to make the perfect risotto."

Again her mind wandered.

Why did everything have to remind her of Josh?

Carmela was cutting up Porcini mushrooms, the best available, for the risotto, the ones she and Josh had picked the day before.

They had gone out early in the morning to gather them and Josh had proved surprisingly adept at identifying them.

"My aunt Paola showed me a long time ago. I nearly got into trouble once when I was a teenager and was over eager. She's normally very easy-going. I added a poisonous one to the mix because I wasn't being careful enough and she told me off in no uncertain terms, telling me I could have killed everyone on the farm and it's a lesson I've never forgotten. So," he grinned at her, "we should be alright apart from the odd death cap. No, only joking," he added. "I really am very, very careful these days."

She had laughed and they had bent over each mushroom, him showing her how to identify each one and her feeling that familiar tingle of excitement as his hand touched hers. "Look, these with the red caps are Russula, the little ones with straight stalks are Chiodini, like little nails, the finferli are what the English call Chanterelles." And so on, the list was endless. She was amazed. She had never realised there were so many kinds of mushrooms.

So now as Carmela was explaining how to heat the risotto rice before adding the stock little by little, she had to once again wrench her thoughts back to the cookery demonstration before they all thought she was half-witted.

Chapter 32

The next few weeks flew by. The hotel was busy, guests came and went and most complimented them, several vowing to return. She took groups to Perugia with its stunning white Priori Palace and wonderful art collection, and to Pienza with another beautiful palace, the Piccolomini, a former summer residence of popes. Then it was time for the Palio in Siena. The famous horse race in Siena was run twice a year, in July and August and Gabriella had purchased tickets for both. The street parties and processions were similar in structure to the Saracen joust in Arezzo, but instead of four quarters competing in a joust for the Golden Lance, Siena had thirteen quarters, ten of which competed in turn in the famous bareback horse race on wild, unbroken horses. Tommaso drove the excited guests towards the city and they parked outside the ancient walls.

Gabriella led her little group through the streets lined with medieval brick buildings, decorated with the flags of each of the contrade, the sections of the city. They arrived at the cathedral, the Duomo, built of striking white and greenish marble, one of Italy's finest, which they duly admired. They lunched at a restaurant near the square, a meal of antipasti, pasta, meat and tiramisu that wonderful dessert which Gabriella translated to the guests as 'Pick me up' made of cream, sugar, biscuits soaked in coffee, eggs and the liqueur that 'picks you up', Marsala wine.

Not that they needed picking up. They could see hordes of excited people rushing towards the square. As soon as the last mouthful of food was eaten, the guests were impatient to get on, so Gabriella led them down through one of the narrow crowded streets to the square and was suitably gratified when they gasped in astonishment. "The square in Siena is perhaps one of the most famous in all of Italy," she explained. "It is a misnomer for a start as it isn't square at all, but a fan shape. It's called the Piazza del Campo, literally 'the square of the field'."

It was lined with beautiful buildings, the focal points being the Palazzo Pubblico, the magnificent town hall, and Torre del Mangia, the enormous tower which faced them as they entered. They found their seats and sat gazing around. The centre of the square barricaded off was filled with excited supporters of the various quarters. "But how will they see what is going on," somebody commented, "packed in like that?"

Gabriella laughed. "It is famously said that the people in the centre 'pay not to see.' Unfortunately, a few people usually faint from the heat and the crush of bodies so you will see them being passed from head to head across to the waiting Red Cross teams."

"Oh dear," someone else commented sympathetically. Then the procession began, glorious in its colour and spectacle. Firstly, a contingent of carabinieri, the mounted police, burst into the square, resplendent in their dress uniforms of scarlet and black. They trotted their beautiful grey horses soberly around the outside ring. Then, to a glorious cheer, they drew their sabres and broke into a furious fast gallop. After that display, the pageant proper got under way. A band in costume circled the piazza, ready to 'play in' each Contrada. All was velvet, fur, gold and silver and rich embroidery. Five hundred participants moved slowly around the square in a ritual lasting two hours. The flag bearers performed their balletic display and Gabriella explained that there was a superstition that the Contrada whose flag was tossed the highest would win the race so each one made a super-human effort.

The Palio itself, a large painted silk banner embroidered with silver coins, was taken down from a cart drawn by four white oxen and then it was hoisted into the air. Many hands reached out to touch it as an omen of good luck. The great bell on the tower tolled, the drums rolled and a mortar was let off, making the pigeons wheel through the sky. Then one of her guests squealed excitedly, "Look the horses are here!"

There were ten of them and lots were drawn with large, coloured wooden marbles, each horse entering the space between two ropes at the start, with the last horse to be drawn starting from the side. They would gallop around the outer rim of the square three times. There was shouting from the crowd, the jockeys and the grooms as the horses bucked, pranced and kicked. Gabriella, horse lover that she was, couldn't help but feel sorry for them. They were totally wild horses, mostly from Sardinia, and had never been broken in and to endure such noise and confusion must have been terrifying. She also had to admire the bravery of the jockeys though, to ride bareback on such mounts. Then the rope went down and they were off, manes and tails streaming in the wind.

One jockey attempted to overtake on the inside of the curve, hit the wooden rails and fell. The horse continued by itself. The whole race was over in a matter of moments. Six horses were in at the thrilling finish, five with jockeys, one without. People were running, screaming. Others were weeping from grief or joy in each other's arms. Gabriella explained that if the riderless horse had come first it would have won even without a jockey. "It's the horse that wins, not the rider," she said.

"Wow, that was amazing," a guest exclaimed. "I realised that I was actually holding my breath the whole time. I simply forgot to breathe; it was so exciting."

"What happens now?" Someone asked.

"The winners go to the cathedral to give thanks. There is a victory dinner and a special risotto is served to each guest from the silver dish from the top of the Palio banner. The horse has a place of honour, with his favourite food also served on a silver plate. The Sienese never forget that the horse is the most important guest of all."

Tommaso drove them home; everyone still chattering excitedly about what they had seen. That night Carmela had made a superb risotto for dinner served on little silvery dishes reminiscent of the Palio and the guests exclaimed in pleasure.

"You are so clever," they said, "to remind us of the wonderful day we have had." And Gabriella looked across the room to find Josh smiling at her. And there was a warmth in his eyes that had never been there before.

****

Things had definitely changed between them. They had become a team. On a professional level, she was learning from him every day. As well as the residents they had started organising private lunch and dinner parties in her father's old library lined with precious books, many of them first editions. They took on more staff, willing workers from the nearby villages and Josh made sure they were trained to serve properly so there were no disasters with food being spilt on the guests in their finery. They had plans to convert one of the barns so they could host bigger functions, large weddings and conferences. Josh got estimates and they pored over them together, heads almost touching. They had wine tastings in cooperation with one of the local vintners.

She was so excited because the list of things they could do and ways they could expand was endless.

Chapter 33

Then they held their first wedding, closing the hotel to everyone except the wedding guests. Gabriella soon learned that her most important job was soothing the mother of the bride, who was so anxious that everything should go well that she was in danger of stressing out the bride herself. The bride, her mother and the bridesmaids met Gabriella beforehand to discuss arrangements for a lavish buffet and Gabriella had given her suggestions from Carmela which they loved. Then they talked about the flowers and the bride's mother had her own rather traditional ideas and hinted strongly that as she was paying for them she should be able to choose. The bride however didn't agree. She wanted a country look, something quite informal and relaxed and it took all Gabriella's skill in diplomacy to settle the matter. On the day itself, the lines of white daisies in pots enchanted the guests and Gabriella and Gianetta had risen early to pick wild flowers from the estate grounds which they arranged in small vases on the tables. The tiny private chapel with its whitewashed walls and hammer beam wooden roof was too small for all the guests to be accommodated inside but it had been agreed that the remainder could be seated outside and the service screened for them.

The bride and groom had the option of a nearby church but loved the idea of the private chapel with only close family inside and didn't think the rest, mostly their young friends, would mind. Josh had arranged an awning and a large screen for the rest of the guests, most of whom were staying in a local agriturismo. They had arrived in cars sporting banners and large white bows on their antennae to indicate a wedding, horns blaring as they raced in exuberant fashion up the drive. She watched the ceremony outside from behind the congregation. It was very touching as both bride and groom shed tears of emotion as they said their vows. She couldn't help but glance across at Josh and saw that he had been glancing at her at the same time but he turned away quickly when he saw her looking. The buffet was laid out in a room just off the terrace and the band played all the old romantic Italian tunes to which the guests danced after the meal and the speeches.

A quartet of elderly men on violins and accordions took over and sang a bawdy song about a couple getting married where, once they retired to their room, the bride took out her glass eye, then her hearing aid and then her wig and so on until the room was rocking with laughter. The guests grew noisier with shouts of 'Bacio!' exhorting the bride and groom to kiss which they obligingly did and there were frequent toasts to the health of the happy couple.

The bride raised her skirts delicately and took off an embroidered garter which she tossed in the air. There were cheers as the man who caught it placed it solemnly on his head. The bonbonieri, the little parcels of sugared almonds, were handed out to signify good luck and finally, late in the evening, the bride and groom were driven away on their honeymoon while the rest of the guests either departed for their agriturismo or went upstairs to their rooms. All in all, it was a good day and as they sank exhausted round Carmela's kitchen table at two o'clock in the morning, finishing off a spare bottle of Prosecco, they raised a glass to each other and Gabriella knew that her hotel was really up and running properly at last and was a success. All being well, they could start to pay off the overdraft very soon.

Chapter 34

Not long afterwards, they had a very inquisitive single woman staying. She dined alone and Gabriella saw her watching attentively every time a dish was served to other customers and she requested things not on the menu which they tried hard to provide.

She began to get an uneasy feeling.

"Josh," she whispered. "I think we have an inspector from one of the food guides."

"Yes, I was coming to the same conclusion," he whispered back.

"Do they always come anonymously?"

"Absolutely…so you are not on your 'best behaviour'. They want to see how you react with the other customers and not put on a special show."

"Should we tell Carmela?"

"Definitely not," he said emphatically. "She's perfectly capable and she will only get flustered. She always turns out delicious food and I haven't known a dish go wrong all the time I've been here."

"We have to be watchful though because I've noticed her asking questions of Marco and Gianetta and she was having a long chat with Rosanna yesterday. I'm sure none of them would say anything silly, but you never know."

Gabriella found the woman, Worthington was her name, out in the kitchen garden, chatting to Sergio the gardener. When she saw Gabriella, she said to Sergio, "Well, I must let you get on with your work," and she switched her attention to Gabriella.

"You haven't been open very long I gather," she said.

"No, only eighteen months."

"You are very young to be running such an establishment."

"Well, I do have some financial experience. I was doing a degree in London in business studies when, well, let's just say my circumstances changed and I came back here. Anyway, I have, as you may have noticed, a very capable manager in Josh."

"Yes, he does seem to be very alert and on the ball."

"Would you like me to show you around the estate and explain what we do here?" Gabriella asked.

"Yes, that would be very kind," the woman replied. "Are all your vegetables organic?"

"Oh yes, we don't use pesticides of any kind. And as you may have noticed, we only serve what is in season at the moment. We get all our meat, ham, sausages and cheeses from local suppliers and other things from the farms around here that grow organically as well." She could almost see the woman's mind mentally ticking off each item as she said it. This was definitely an inspector.

They walked down past the field of sunflowers. "Very Tuscan," the woman commented.

"Yes, glorious, aren't they? So full of hope and happiness; a feeling we like to inspire here in our hotel." She showed Miss Worthington where they pressed the olives and wandered on through the olive grove.

"We make all our own olive oil ...extra extra virgin of course."

"You don't have any diseases on your trees?"

"Mercifully not. Sadly, the Xylella disease is affecting some of the trees in Puglia but hasn't reached our part of Tuscany yet. Our estate manager Antonio keeps a watchful eye out though."

Then there were the grapes, luscious and sweet and almost ready to be picked.

"Everyone comes to help at harvest time and we have a huge supper afterwards for all the helpers."

"It sounds idyllic."

They wandered back up to the Castello, diverting for a few moments in order for Gabriella to introduce her to Tosca who was in her field and who whinnied a welcome as they approached. Gabriella could see that the woman was fond of horses and was tempted to tell her about her plans to ride in the joust but thought better of it. Instead, she spoke of her plans to show guests the marvels of Tuscany and enthused about the wonderful villages and relatively unknown places as well as the big cities.

They walked back; then Miss Worthington said, "Your food is delicious. May I meet your chef? I think it's a woman."

"Yes," Gabriella replied. "Carmela has been with us for a long time, since before I was born. Her food, as you may have noticed, is not fancy. Just good typical Tuscan dishes."

Her heart was beating slightly as she led the woman into the kitchen. It would have been just her luck to go in just as a rare catastrophe had occurred and someone had dropped a pan but thankfully, all was serene and calm as usual with Carmela and Lucia preparing pasta and sauces for the evening meal.

"Excuse us, Carmela, but one of our guests has asked to see who makes all of these delicious meals."

Carmella flushed with pleasure, dusted her hands on her apron shook hands and then before turning back to the pasta, washed them very carefully. Gabriella saw the woman making a mental note and her eagle eyes scanned the kitchen, noticing the gleaming copper pots, the tidy wood-fired range and the array of freshly picked salads and vegetables being washed and prepared by Lucia.

Finally, she said, "Thank you. I must let you get on now."

"No, it's been a pleasure," Gabriella said, "I'm always happy to show people what we do here."

Then the woman turned and beamed. "Yes, for me too…it has been most interesting."

She sounded sincere and Gabriella could only hope that if she really was an inspector for a Food Guide she really meant it and had been impressed by what she saw.

Time would tell.

As it was, they were already getting rave reviews in local publications and TripAdvisor and diners were clamouring for tables and rooms from all over the local area. They only had one negative review and when Josh investigated it turned out to be Domenico and he got it removed very speedily.

Josh was busy with training the extra staff they had taken on, making sure they served correctly, were smartly dressed and also that they knew about the food they were serving so they could recommend dishes and answer any queries the guests had. He himself always took charge of the wine. Guests were keen to try the local light white fruity wine from the estate and recent vintages had been very good so it was very popular.

Several months later, Gabriella received a parcel through the post. It was a copy of a guide to the 'Best places to eat and stay in Tuscany'.

In mounting excitement, she opened the book at the first page.

She didn't have far to look.

'A jewel in the crown of Tuscany' went the headline. 'Small and intimate but all the better for it'. They had been voted Number One with a glowing review on the quality and freshness of the food. Tuscan food at its best, read the byline. It also praised the comfort, the ambience and the friendliness of the staff.

And not only that, there was a slip of paper inside saying, "I don't usually write to the owners of the places I visit but you will see I was incredibly impressed by your passion, commitment, enthusiasm and dedication. Keep going. Best wishes Isabel Worthington."

Josh came into the office.

"What is it?" He asked, seeing her shining face.

"Do you remember the woman we thought was an inspector?"

"Yes.?"

"Well, she was." She held out the book open at the front page. And the note.

He glanced down to read, then raised his face to hers, his face also alight with pleasure. "Incredible," he said with a broad grin. "We must be doing something right."

She couldn't help it. She ran forwards and embraced him and he didn't resist. She could smell his aftershave and feel the softness of his hair on her cheek. She hugged him for a brief moment then reluctantly let him go.

"Now," she said, gathering her composure together again. "Now we must go and tell Carmela and the rest of the staff and have a glass of something to celebrate."

Chapter 35

The wild boar were among the grapes.

Antonio came rushing up to the house to warn them all to be careful and especially to keep Lupo on the lead.

The guests were intrigued.

"I've never seen a wild boar. Can we go and have a look?" One said and several others were eager to go as well.

"It's not wise," Josh said. "They are incredibly dangerous animals and can inflict nasty bites, not to mention their sharp tusks. Whatever you do, don't go near them."

But some guests insisted on going down to the vineyard. It was dusk, the time when the animals usually came out to forage. Josh and Gabriella went with them to ensure no harm came to anyone. Gabriella had Lupo on a lead and as they got nearer he began to growl.

She gathered the guests at a safe distance on a small mound looking down on the scene. They could hear low grunts and the sound of snuffling as the pack of four adult males moved through the rows of grapes. They could see their large bodies covered in grey-brown bristly fur with long hard snouts, little white tusks visibly protruding.

"Their sight is weak but their sense of smell and sound is very strong," Gabriella explained, keeping her voice low. "They forage from dusk till dawn and the largest one ever recorded was 150 kilos, so please don't try to go any nearer. You will notice that they shake their tail when they are annoyed and raise their mane to make themselves look more aggressive. They dig themselves shallow burrows and then rub themselves against the trunks of trees to remove the mud."

"How long do they live?" Someone asked.

"Anywhere between ten and thirty years," Gabriella replied.

Tommaso and Antonio were both there with their guns but there was to be no shooting that evening, much to the disappointment of one of the guests.

"Official hunting season is November to January," Gabriella continued, "but we are allowed to shoot them if they are damaging our crops."

"I hear they've become quite a pest in Italian cities now," said one guest.

"That's right, Rome particularly," Gabriella replied. "There's a huge argument going on as to whether they're allowed to be culled or not because they have become so widespread and are beyond a nuisance, even causing accidents because they wander all over the roads, especially at night, searching for food."

"But the piglets are so cute when they're little," said one of the women guests, "little ginger things with cream stripes."

"Yes, that camouflages them in the undergrowth," Gabriella explained, "but then like nearly all animals they are not so cute when they are fully grown."

"But they make great sauce," said another guest with a laugh. "Your cook is very good with them."

Gabriella smiled. "Yes, Carmela says the sauce is even more flavoursome when the boars have been at the grapes but I don't think Antonio wants to let them loose on our own crop."

In the meantime, Antonio and Tommaso between them had managed to drive the boars away without shooting them and were busy repairing the fence.

"So we won't be getting any of them for supper," said one disappointed guest.

"Don't worry, there's a plentiful supply of salsa di cingiale, boar sauce," Josh put in, "and salami and prosciutto too, so you won't starve."

"Tuscany is still a haven for a lot of other wildlife too," Gabriella added. "We have wolves, deer, hares, foxes, pheasants and even porcupines."

"Really?" A guest said. "I didn't know you had wolves."

"Yes, they were introduced partly to cull the boars but of course that's another story as they are becoming a problem too, taking other small animals."

"Isn't that the name of your dog? Lupo…isn't that wolf in Italian?"

"Yes it is but he's not one." Gabriella laughed. "He's quite tame. When we get back, you can stroke him."

So, drama over, she and Josh led the little party back up to the Castello, and by great good fortune it was cingiale al pappardelle, pasta with boar sauce, on the menu that night.

Chapter 36

It was time to take the plunge. She had put it off long enough.

She walked along the road past the ivy-covered stone walls and into the Piazza Porta Crucifera, hung with the banners of the quarter. She climbed the steps to the headquarters, her heart beating fast.

She took a deep breath to calm her nerves

The Rettore rose to greet her as she entered his office.

"I'm sorry to interrupt you," she began, "but I was just passing."

"Gabriella!" he replied coming forward and embracing her. "How wonderful to see you. I have heard great things about your new venture. You must tell me all about it."

She knew him well. He was middle-aged now but in her father's day he had been vice Rettore, a fresh-faced young man while she was just a small child and he had taken over when the old Rettore had retired. It wasn't a full-time job of course; all the positions of the various quarters were honorary ones, helped by other honorary positions such as the captains, the secretaries, the committees to help with various projects that looked after the widows the orphans and others in need. It even had a youth committee, among them no doubt future captains and rectors.

" Sit, sit and tell me what you have been doing and how my friend Antonio is doing."

She sat in the proffered chair and while she filled him on all the changes at the Castello she gazed around her. As well as his office it was, as with all the quarters, a museum of costumes through the ages. There was a board inscribed with all the victories and the famous riders itemised, including the five victories of her father. There were the steel helmets of the captains, the lances which had won the joust, the flags and crests and the targets with the black marks where the lance had struck the bullseye. They were all arranged in the front office and in serried ranks in the corridor behind him. Above his head were photographs of

138

the victorious riders, her father's among them. As she gazed at his handsome, smiling, youthful face, she wrenched her eyes away as she felt a jolt of strong emotion.

There too was the crest of the quarter, one half red and decorated with a cross, the other half green with a design of the campanile, the bell tower of the Pieve in the square.

He offered her a cup of coffee which she accepted to steady her nerves.

The pleasantries over, there was a moment of silence.

Gazing at her the Rettore asked, "But I think if I am not mistaken, there is a specific reason you have come here today. Are you in need of help because if there is anything we can do…?" His voice tailed off.

She took another deep breath and said, "I wish to take part in the joust."

"But of course," he said. "I am sure we can find a place for you in the procession. You can walk with the ladies. I can speak to their committee. I am sure they will fit you in an appropriate dress. The velvet gowns are very becoming."

"No," Gabriella replied, "I think you misunderstand me. I wish to be considered as one of the riders for the quarter."

There was a moment when it seemed the Rettore was going to pass out. His complexion changed from a healthy tan, to white, to pink and again back to white.

"But, but, Gabriella," he spluttered, "it is not possible."

"Is there anything in the constitution of the joust that says a woman can't ride?"

"Well, I honestly don't know," he blurted out. "I suppose it has always been a man."

She could see he was desperately trying to think of reasons why he couldn't accommodate this mad request and finally lighted on one.

"The lance is very heavy," he said. "Too heavy for a woman."

"I know it is heavy," she said, "but I have been practising, not with a proper lance but with the equivalent weight of a long branch and it depends on the way you hold it. If you are able to, I would like you to come and see me practise, something I have been doing for the past year almost every day."

"My god, Gabriella, you do put me in a difficult position," he retorted. "There are many, in fact, nearly all of the committee, who are traditionalists and they would never stand for it."

Gabriella though was nothing if not persistent.

"But I would still like to put my name forward. Perhaps some of the committee could come as well one day and watch me ride?"

"Well, I suppose they could," he said reluctantly. "Ordinarily, I would turn you down flat but I have to say your father's name is a part of our history in the quarter and we have to respect that and give you a chance to show what you can do."

"Thank you," said Gabriella.

She rose from her seat.

"May I take it then that you will be in touch?"

"Yes, yes of course," he said weakly.

She smiled at him and waited as he rose to his feet and moved quickly to open the door to his office as if he couldn't wait to get rid of her fast enough.

"Thank you," she said as she went through and down the steps. She almost skipped along through the Piazza Porta Crucifera underneath the banners.

She had taken the first step. Now all she had to do was to prove to them that she really could do it, that a woman really could take part in the joust. And maybe even win it.

Chapter 37

They came, of course, the committee and she could see it was reluctantly. They were prepared, perhaps, to sneer. But they had to humour her.

They stood in a group at the side of the field. The Rettore had given her a lance, a proper one and she had practised with it every morning for three weeks. Antonio was watching from the sidelines and he and the Rettore embraced affectionately and reminisced for a while about the old days.

Then it was time for the business of the day.

Tosca, it seemed, was on wings that morning as if she sensed what was at stake. Gabriella had set up a target and she urged the horse into a canter, then a gallop. She concentrated as she had never concentrated before…and she succeeded.

After the first run, she hit a three.

She could hear murmurs of surprise.

Then she wheeled Tosca around and went back to the start for another run.

And this time, she hit the dead centre.

A five.

There was a silence and she could see that despite themselves, they were impressed. She glanced over at Antonio standing on the opposite side of the field and saw him smile and nod in approval at her as she trotted back.

"Well done, Gabriella," the Rettore said reluctantly. "But of course, there are other factors involved, the noise of the crowd, the Buratta swinging the metal chains."

"Yes," Gabriella agreed. "I have already thought of that. I will record the crowd noises and play them to get Tosca used to the noise and I'm sure Antonio can help me manufacture a model of the Buratta." She glanced over at him and he nodded.

So she had made her point and as they said their farewells, she could see a new respect in their eyes.

All that remained now was the opportunity to prove herself at the joust.

Chapter 38

Even though the hotel was busy, she still managed to get time to practise, galloping towards the glorious skies of the sunrise on the distant horizon. The joust was due soon but she had given up any hope that they would call her. They would be taking too much of a risk with an untried rider. She still practised endlessly though, rising at dawn each day to take Tosca out.

It seemed that the horse too was looking forward eagerly to showing what she could do as she whickered softly when Gabriella arrived each day as if to say, 'Here you are at last. When can we start?'

A call came at last. "Buon giorno, Gabriella." It was the Rettore. Her heart leapt. This was it. He was asking her to ride!

"About your wish to ride in the joust," he paused. She was tense with excitement. " I'm afraid we have selected our riders for this coming year. Two excellent young men who have proved their worth in the past. I am sorry, Gabriella, but I think the quarter is not ready for a female rider. Maybe sometime in the future."

"I understand," she blurted out, "but thank you anyway for considering me. I really appreciate it." She ended the call and stood for a moment, devastation sweeping over her. What had she been thinking? That they would overturn years of tradition for a mere girl? An untried one at that. She must have been mad! Nevertheless, tears of disappointment sprang into her eyes which she angrily brushed away. She needed comfort and where would she find that? With Tosca, of course. She slipped out of the back door and went to the stable where Tosca waited. She buried her head in the horse's mane and cried. All those months of practising for nothing. There was a movement in the door of the stable block.

"Gabriella, oh there you are…oh, are you ok?" It was Josh. He came towards her. " What's the matter? Have you had bad news?" His face was a picture of concern.

"No, well, it's nothing really." She told him about the Rettore's call. He looked at her in astonishment.

"You really hoped to ride in the joust?" He said, "I mean, I know you've been practising, but those riders…they are professional, aren't they?" Gabriella was instantly furious.

"What do you mean 'they are professional'? Yes, they are experienced but they don't do it for money, no one does. They do it for the glory of the quarter. I got on my first pony when I was two and I've been riding ever since. I've been getting up every day at dawn to practise and I have scored well. The committee gave me a lance so I could practise properly. They were considering me, they really were." She was shouting now.

"Ok, ok. I'm sorry," he said, chastened. "Please don't shout at me." She was still furious.

"You think I'm stupid, don't you, for even trying? Well, one day I will succeed, just you wait. You think you know it all, don't you, you men? You are so full of yourselves." She ran towards him and beat her fists on his chest and he ducked to avoid her flailing arms.

"Gabriella," he was almost shouting in return. "Gabriella, I'm sorry. I didn't realise it meant so much to you. I thought it was just a hobby. Please forgive me." Her face was streaked in tears as she stood back and he tenderly wiped them from her cheeks. "I'm sorry," he said again.

Then the floodgates opened and all the emotion, all the feelings she had for him, came pouring out.

"Oh Josh, why do you have to be so stubborn?" She raged. "All this fuss about the Castello and my title. Don't you realise how much I need you? I would be nothing, this place would be nothing without you. I would have to sell up to some rich plutocrat who would fill it with glitz and tat and probably get rid of the vines to make a race track. You have made so much difference, don't you see that? By the end of the year, we will be making money." She took a deep breath. A thought came to her out of nowhere. Without pausing even to think, she blurted out, "I want you to be my official partner in the hotel, whatever happens to us personally. I will put your name on the deeds."

He drew back and looked hard into her face, in amazement. "You really mean that? You are not just reacting about your disappointment over the joust?"

"I really mean it, Josh," she said, her voice stronger and more convinced. It had actually not occurred to her before but once she had said it, she had no regrets. It would be an ideal situation.

Then she had a moment of panic. What was she saying? A moment ago, she was telling him that men were awful, so full of themselves, then she had done a complete volte-face and told him that he, a man, was the only person who could help her. No matter. Whatever happened between them personally, he was the man who would make the hotel a success and she needed him. If making him a partner in the business was what it took, so be it. Her romantic feelings were something else entirely. She thought he would jump at the chance, but instead he hesitated. "It's a wonderful offer but let me think about it."

"Alright," she said. She now realised that in offering him a partnership, he would think she was also trying to buy his affection. The offer had been made so spontaneously and maybe that had in fact been at the back of her mind when she said it; that they would be partners in real life as well as in business. Was she in fact trying to snare him that way if she couldn't get him any other way?

"I'll let you know," was all he said. Then he turned and walked out the door, leaving her gazing after him in frustration.

Chapter 39

Food was going missing.

Gabriella had been having her morning coffee with Carmela in the kitchen when Carmela suddenly said, "I don't want to worry you but I think someone is stealing food. It's not much, the odd pie here and there or a cake or two. I thought at first I was mistaken and had forgotten I'd that I'd used it but Lucia has noticed the same thing so I know I'm not wrong."

She hesitated then continued. "I don't want to accuse someone without proof but I'm pretty sure it coincides with the times Rosa and Nella are here."

Gabriella frowned. Rosa and Nella were the two cleaning ladies who came from the village, sometimes together if they were really busy, or sometimes separately.

"I'll speak to Josh," she said to Carmela. "It's obviously a delicate matter because we can't accuse either of them without proof."

"Of course not," Carmela said, "and it will be sad if it is one of them. They are both hard-working, pleasant ladies and I know they need the money but I can't think who else it could be."

Gabriella spoke to Josh, telling him who Carmela suspected.

" I see," he said slowly. "You're right, it is an awkward one. Carmela and Lucia are both in the kitchen most of the time so the food must be taken when they're out in the kitchen garden gathering the salads and vegetables for the day."

In the end, the mystery was easily solved as Josh watched when the two cleaning ladies were in the bar and Carmela and Lucia went out together to gather enough vegetables for the evening meal. He saw Rosa walk away on the pretext that she was going to the bathroom and then slip into the kitchen with her bag.

He caught her red-handed with a custard tart that Lucia had made for the guests that evening.

When she saw she had been caught, she burst into tears and started wailing. "O Dio Mio, no, no, no. I didn't mean it, please forgive me. Please don't sack me. I promise not to do it again. I promise, I promise."

Josh sat her down on a chair at the kitchen table and gestured to Carmela and Lucia to stay out of the room as they were hovering in the doorway. He could see Carmela was crying in sympathy with Rosa.

"Tell me," he said gently, "why you have been taking food?"

Rosa was sobbing noisily into her apron, almost incoherent, and kept saying, "Mi dispiace, mi dispiace. I'm sorry, I'm sorry, please don't sack me. Please, please, please. I need the money," again and again.

Eventually, her sobs subsided and Josh found her a tissue to wipe her face and blow her nose.

Then it all poured out. She had three small children and her husband had abandoned her. She didn't know where he had gone and she had no money other than that she earned cleaning for the Castello and a few other local jobs. By the time she paid the rent on her room and for clothes for the children, she had very little money left for food.

She was now sitting silently apart from the odd hiccupping sob, head down despairingly like a prisoner awaiting the death sentence.

Josh said quietly, "Rosa, whatever your circumstances...and I sympathise... there is no excuse for stealing. I will however speak to Gabriella and let you know what we decide. I think it's better you go home now and let Nella finish the cleaning. You're in no fit state to carry on."

Rosa departed, stumbling out with a final plea to be forgiven and a promise that she would never ever steal again and please, please not to sack her.

So he spoke to Gabriella and it didn't take long for her to come to a decision.

"I think in the circumstances, we give her a second chance. There is no way she would steal from us again now we know. It's a sad case though. Poor woman. How can a man go off like that and leave his children to go hungry? I'd like to ring his neck." She was appalled.

"I'm so glad you said that," Josh replied. "I'll find out where she lives and go and tell her. We must keep the whole episode quiet though. I'm sure Carmela and Lucia won't say anything. I don't want the rest of the staff to know."

So Rosa came back to work the next day looking very shamefaced and subdued and nothing else was said about what had happened.

Then two days later, Gabriella was out taking Lupo for his usual walk through the estate. She went through the flourishing kitchen garden lined with all manner of vegetables, salads and herbs. She had a brief chat with Sergio the gardener busily tending the rows of courgettes and lettuces. She admired the abundance of ripe tomatoes and watermelons, then she went through into the orchard where she could see healthy crops of apples, pears, oranges and lemons and figs.

She sighed with pleasure at nature's bounty.

Then she went along the side of the fields full of sunflowers, their heads now turning brown and almost ready for the seed to be collected and sold. Then she was on the edge of the vineyard where Antonio and his men were busy stripping away some of the foliage on the rows of vines to make harvesting the grapes much easier. She waved and was continuing on her way across the fields when she noticed a figure in front of her walking purposefully along carrying two shopping bags.

It was Josh.

Out of curiosity, she followed him at a safe distance. He didn't turn but she realised he was heading towards the local village. A thought came into her mind. Where could he possibly be going but to see Rosa?

She carried on walking enjoying the still warm autumn air while Lupo ran before her busily investigating every rock and tree. Eventually, she turned around and walked back towards the Castello and there was Josh again, this time without the bags.

She didn't want him to see her or to think she was following him so she hung back. But Lupo had other ideas. He ran forward and Josh looked down, surprised at finding the dog beside him. He turned around and saw Gabriella.

"Oh hi," he said. "Where did you spring from?"

"Ciao," she said casually. "We're just out for a walk."

He hesitated. Then he said, "Me too."

She decided to take the plunge. "Have you been to the village?" She inquired casually.

"Yes."

He didn't he obviously didn't want to divulge any more information.

Then he changed his mind and confessed, "Ok then. I went to see Rosa. I was worried about her. I saw the other day where she lives and how she lives."

His face was working with emotion. "Oh, Gabriella," he burst out, "it's awful. She has these three small children …the oldest must be about eight. They have hardly any furniture and they live in one room with only two beds. The children look malnourished and are dressed in rags. No wonder she stole food. I think her wages from us and a few other small jobs she has are the only money she gets. So I went to give her some food. Not from us," he hastened to add.

"No, no," Gabriella assured him. "I would never think that. But of course, we must help her," she continued. "Why didn't it occur to me? I'm embarrassed. We always have food left over even after we have fed the staff and there is always a glut of vegetables in the kitchen garden."

"Oh thank you," he said. "I didn't like to ask."

"Don't be silly. It's the least we can do. I know my father always looked after the local people, anyone who was in trouble. He made it his business to find out and help whenever he could. I just didn't think about it after he died. We may have our difficulties keeping up the house and the estate but it's a ridiculous problem compared with what some people have to put up with just to survive."

Then she added, "Thank you, Josh, for making me see what I should have done before. I was so preoccupied with my own worries about the Castello; it never occurred to me to think about how things were for people outside the estate."

"Well, don't blame yourself," he said. "You have done miracles in order to keep the estate workers in employment and also to provide the local farmers and other suppliers with an extra income."

So, decision made, they walked in companionable silence with Lupo bounding ahead until they reached the Castello, Gabriella thinking that Rosa's problems had somehow brought them closer together. Pondering someone else's feelings rather than her own meant she had no time to dwell on what felt like a hopeless love for the man beside her who had shown how wonderfully tender-hearted and caring he was.

And Rosa…

The very next day she came in to clean, still unable to look Gabriella in the eyes.

Just before she left, Josh called her into the kitchen.

Her expression was one of terror, worried that despite what he had said before, she was going to be sacked after all.

"It's alright," he said gently, "no need to worry. It's just that Gabriella and I have talked about your situation and we want to help. We will give you vegetables from the garden and any spare food that Carmela feels she can't use. We don't want your children to go hungry."

And Rosa burst into tears and clung to him. "Grazie mille, Grazie, how can I ever thank you enough?"

Josh awkwardly extracted himself from Rosa's tearful embrace and glancing over at Gabriella who was standing in the doorway, smiled a smile of genuine affection and respect and her heart leapt with hope. But then even the next day things changed yet again so what was she to believe?

Chapter 40

Gabriella was happy and relaxed. They were sitting by the pool in Josh's aunt Paola's agriturismo enjoying the last of the late summer sun. She had been surprised and delighted when Josh had come to her and said, "I want to ask you something." Excitement had welled up in her. Maybe he was considering her offer. Instead, he said "My aunt is having a small party to celebrate her big birthday. My mother and father are flying over and would like to meet you. My aunt and uncle would be delighted if you would come too."

"Tell them I'm honoured to accept…that is if it is ok for both of us to leave on the same day."

"I've checked already," Josh replied. "There are only three guests and they plan to be out for the day. They will be back for dinner but Carmela and Lucia will look after them." So here she was, eyes closed, enjoying the sunshine. It had been a lovely lunch, one of those long leisurely meals sitting at a big table with a few of his aunt and uncle's friends under a vine-covered pergola, listening to amiable chatter and eating food mostly produced from the farm. She hadn't had a chance to relax like this for a very long time and had almost forgotten what it felt like to be carefree for the day. She had been allowed to help Paola in the kitchen, stuffing courgette flowers with ricotta cheese and herbs, dipping them in batter and frying them in oil while they chatted amiably. It was actually fun being able to do some cooking because, with Carmela in charge, she was rarely allowed in the kitchen at the Castello.

She realised with a start that she felt completely at home in the agriturismo, especially with Paola, someone she had found she could talk freely with. She had been introduced to Josh's parents who lived in Hampshire. They were both teachers. His father Eric was head of a village primary school and his mother, Mara, taught Italian at the nearby adult education college. They were both delightful, easy to talk to and interested in how she came to start the hotel. She had explained the circumstances; how she had been studying in London when she had been called back because her father had died. Josh's mother had leaned forward spontaneously to touch her hand. "I am so sorry," she said. "But you are very courageous to start such a venture on your own."

"But I am not alone," Gabriella smiled. "I have your son to help me. I couldn't do without him and that's the truth." Mara smiled at the compliment.

"Yes, we are proud of him. He always wanted a career with people, something that would be different every day. 'Mamma,' he always said, 'I do not want to be stuck in an office staring at the same wall all the time.' I thought at one time he might go into teaching, follow in our footsteps, but I think it suits him, the hotel life."

"And I have found it suits me as well," Gabriella said. "Always fresh challenges. Sometimes too many," she laughed, "but on the whole, it is exciting meeting new people and trying to make them happy, showing off the wonderful Tuscan countryside and all it has to offer in the way of food and wine." After lunch, she had left Josh talking to his parents and wandered off among the olive trees. Josh's aunt Paola found her there gazing out at the view. She came up to her and tucked her arm through Gabriella's. "You don't mind?"

"Of course not. You have such a beautiful place here."

"Not as wonderful as yours I suspect, although I have never seen it."

"You must come, all of you."

"That would be lovely." She hesitated. "He has told us all about your very generous offer." Gabriella looked at her.

"It is not generous at all. I need his help. Without him, I couldn't manage to do what we do. It seemed a simple thing to open up my house to paying guests but I have found there is so much more to it than that, the constant ordering of supplies, the rules and regulations, health and safety inspections, the accounts, staff problems if someone is ill and can't come in. You must know how hard it is sometimes."

"Yes indeed, though on a smaller scale than you of course."

"But I have Antonio who runs the estate for me. You have to do all the farm work as well I think. Do you have help with that?"

"Oh yes, old Giovanni who has worked for us for many years, and neighbours who come in for the olive harvest and the vendemmia, the wine, though we have to help them out as well. Of course, our work is seasonal, we don't open in winter so I have time to catch up. You are open all the year round I think?"

"Yes, though there are obviously going to be quiet times. Some people think that Italy is sunny all year round and are surprised to find it cold and rainy in January and February, so I think we might close then."

Paola was scrutinising her.

"What is it?" Gabriella asked.

"You know when Josh said you were," she hesitated, "well, who you are, we were expecting someone altezzosa, you know?"

Gabriella laughed. "Snooty, you mean?"

"Well, yes."

"I don't think I would have lasted long as a student if I had put on airs and graces. I had no mother, she died when I was born so I lived in a mostly man's world. She wasn't one of the so-called nobility anyway; she was the daughter of one of the estate workers. My father brought me up to remember that we are all equal and to respect my fellow human beings for what they are, not what they have."

Paola nodded, "A wise man indeed."

"He was."

"You must miss him."

"I do, very much."

"But I'm sure he would have been proud of what you are doing."

"I hope so."

Then she gathered her thoughts together, "But Paola…may I call you Paola?"

"Of course."

"You said Josh has told you of my offer? Do you think he will accept it?"

"He will be a fool if he didn't," Paola smiled, "and not just for the job. There is more than the job between you I think?"

Gabriella fought hard to be composed. "Yes," she admitted. She was silent for a moment and Paola waited. "Did he tell you how we met?"

"When he applied for the job?"

"No, before that." She began the now familiar story as if repeating it would make a fairy tale beginning to lead to a fairy tale ending. "I was on my way to a lecture in London with a friend on the London Underground and we were laughing and joking and she asked me who would be my ideal man and…"

"…you saw Josh!"

"Exactly. I looked across the carriage and it seems ridiculous now and on an impulse, I said, 'Just like that man over there'."

153

"Madonna!" Paola clapped her hands in glee. "So what happened next?"

"Well, he heard us, he looked across at me and something clicked, I think for both of us. Then the train stopped and he got up to leave and my friend Flick chased after him to give him my number. He says he really was coming back to give me his." She stopped at the painful memory.

"So?" Paola said. "Please go on."

"He says he rang but that night I got a call that my father had had a stroke and I rushed back here just in time before he died. And then of course I never went back to London."

"Oh, I am sorry," Paola said soberly. Then she grew excited again. "But then he heard about the job from your friend and applied. It is destino." She paused and gazed at Gabriella and asked, "Then why are you not together?"

"Because he is too proud!" Gabriella burst out. "He didn't realise when he came about the fact that I owned the Castello and rubbish about me being a Contessa. I have told him over and over again that my title is nothing, that I will lose the Castello if it is not a success, but still he hangs back. I feel a fool because I have made my feelings for him very obvious, too obvious perhaps."

"Ah, I see the problem. He does not like people to think he wants you for what you are and what they think you have."

"Exactly. So how do I convince him? How can I make him change his mind? Can you speak to him? He values your opinion I can see."

"I do not think that it wise," Paola said slowly. "He has to make up his own mind. As you say, he is proud which is why he is such an honourable person. But love will find a way I think. Do not give up," she looked into Gabriella's face.

They walked on a little way until Paola said finally, "Come, let us go back to the others. They will wonder where we are." They walked, still linked arm in arm, back towards the group sitting under the pergola. Josh looked up enquiringly as they approached and seeing his aunt looking at him was confused for a moment by the expression on her face of slight exasperation. They drove home much later, having agreed that the family would come for lunch the following Sunday.

"That was a lovely day," Gabriella said. "I like your mother and father."

"And I think you like my aunt Paola too."

"Very much," Gabriella smiled, "she is a very wise woman. I feel have found a kindred spirit." They went upstairs together and lingered on the landing outside her bedroom door but finally Josh said, without looking at her, " Goodnight,' and went off to his own room. She could have screamed! Instead, she threw her shoes across the room in frustration.

She threw them very hard indeed.

Chapter 41

At the end of the summer, she took a group to the Sagra in the local village.

"What on earth is a Sagra?" Someone asked.

"I suppose you could call it something like a harvest festival in England, but usually it's a celebration of one particular kind of food. No need to dress up. It's all very relaxed. We'll sit on benches at trestle tables and get served by the locals."

"A bit like those street parties before the joust you were talking about?"

"Exactly," Gabriella replied. "Nothing fancy, everything on paper plates, served by all the volunteers from the village."

Tommaso drove them as usual in the minibus and as they entered the narrow streets of the village they could already hear the music.

Tommaso parked and they walked around the corner. "Wow, what a sight. Looks like everyone in the village is here," they said.

Gabriella had bought tickets. "It's first come, first served," she explained. "The money goes towards community projects and everyone gives their services free."

"Sounds good."

"Now we can all sit together or you can mingle with the locals. It's up to you. I'm sure some of the villagers, especially the young ones, would be delighted to try out their languages on you. Oh and there will be dancing later."

She gave out the tickets. "You will need these to get your food," she explained. A few of the more adventurous guests went off to mingle with the villagers.

"It's a Sagra of mushrooms, this one, and I think you'll find nearly everything you eat, apart from the dessert, will have mushrooms in it. But don't worry," she saw one man's expression, "there will be alternatives if you really hate them."

Her little group sat down and she glanced around. Josh was also there as it was his evening off but he had elected to join the fun and he was already in animated conversation with the group of young people at the next table.

She sighed. She would have loved to have sat next to him but she had to remind herself that she was on duty and had to look after her guests.

The food arrived as predicted on paper plates, mushroom crostini to start, mixed mushrooms on slices of toasted bread served by a nervous teenager biting his lip in concentration in case he dropped anything. They were served wine in paper cups.

"This is the local wine, made here from the grapes grown on the hill up there." She pointed to where serried lines of vines grew on the hillside above them.

"Not bad at all," they said approvingly, reaching to fill their cups again from the central flask.

Pasta with mushroom sauce was next to arrive, again served by the same nervous teenager. She smiled at him and said something in Italian to him.

"Grazie," he replied.

"What did you say?" A guest asked curiously.

"It's just that he was doing a really good job. I don't think he's been a waiter before."

"You can tell," they laughed.

Cake came next and she glanced over at Josh again. He was talking in an animated fashion to the girl next to him, a rather attractive blonde who reached over and stroked his hair.

For a moment, she was struck with such a violent attack of jealousy that she could scarcely breathe and she tried desperately to tear her eyes away from the sight of the two of them.

The meal over; the dancing began.

The centre of the square was cleared and a kind of communal dance took place with old and young mingling in long lines, moving side to side, backwards and forwards, turning together and clapping as they turned. Grandmothers danced with granddaughters and even great-granddaughters, grandfathers too, uncles with nieces, aunts with nephews ,age was no barrier.

"Come on, let's go," said a guest, grabbing his wife and off they went to join one of the lines. Another guest offered his hand to Gabriella and they followed the first couple. She tried hard to look animated and as if she was having fun but she couldn't help a surreptitious glance over to where Josh and the blonde girl were now dancing together and laughing.

She felt sick.

"Are you ok?" The man asked.

"Yes fine," she tried to sound cheerful. "One too many plates of mushrooms, I think." And concentrated on keeping up a bright line of chatter with him.

The whole evening had become torture. Try as she might, she couldn't help catching sight of them dancing, laughing and she could see the girl was constantly touching him at every opportunity.

It ended finally after what seemed like an eternity and she shepherded the happy group back towards the minibus where Tommaso waited.

"What a wonderful evening! I feel like this has been the real Italy," somebody gushed.

Gabriella forced a smile.

"You Italians certainly know how to party!" someone else said and then added, "And that young manager of yours was having a good time too. The girl he was with couldn't keep her hands off him."

She felt as if a knife had twisted in her heart. She had never felt an emotion like it before.

She escorted them all back into the hotel and several of them embraced her. "Thank you, thank you for such a great time."

Four of the guests then wanted to stay up and have a nightcap. There was no one else on duty so it was up to her to fetch the drinks for them.

"Stay and sit with us," they begged. "Tell us more about the local customs."

So she was forced to sit and appear animated for a further hour as they plied her with questions.

And the worst of it was that Josh still hadn't appeared. Was he still partying or, worse, had he gone home with the girl?

The guests went to bed at last and she was able to escape to her room. Too overwrought to cry, she lay sleepless until at last she heard faint footsteps creeping along the landing.

Josh was back. At least he hadn't spent the night with her.

The following morning she was up early and trying again to greet the guests with a cheerful, "Good morning." Most of them luckily were either late down or had ordered breakfast in their rooms and Gianetta was kept busy carrying trays upstairs.

Josh appeared at last.

"Good morning," he said cheerfully.

Gabriella tried to keep her voice level. "Good morning. I see you had fun last night."

She had tried hard to keep her tone neutral but there must have been something in her voice that reflected her feelings.

He looked at her and smiled.

"Well, we said we were keeping to a professional relationship, didn't we?"

"Yes, yes of course. I didn't mean…" her voice tailed off.

"Well then," he said, "we'd better get on with our work."

Chapter 42

Gabriella didn't have time to brood about the night before because on the estate it was the busiest time of the year.

Antonio had, of course, been pacing for weeks. It reminded her of films she had seen when fathers, before they had been allowed to watch the birth, impatiently paced up and down outside the bedroom, waiting for the son and heir to arrive.

Every time he appeared in the kitchen doorway for his mid-morning coffee, Carmela looked up hopefully, but each time he shook his head.

For Antonio, at this time of the year, there was no rest. First of all it was the vendemmia—the grape harvest. Friends and neighbours would be summoned because, in this tight community of estates and farms, everyone helped everyone else.

It wasn't until a full week later that he announced that the Castello grapes were finally just right. He came into the kitchen with a triumphant look. "Andiamo," he said. "Let's go."

Everything to do with the wine making, of course, had to be scrupulously clean, and all the equipment was scrubbed within an inch of its life.

Curious guests came to watch the tractor trundle down to the vineyard, and buckets were put out for the grapes.

"Why are there roses planted at the end of each row?" someone asked.

Gabriella explained that they were a kind of early warning system. "They attract insects before the vines. They also get fungal disease like black rot and mildew before the vines."

"Oh , not just for decoration then?"

"No," Gabriella laughed. "Not just for decoration."

Some of them wanted to lend a hand but soon found it was back breaking work: moving along the rows, cutting the huge bunches and putting them in the buckets.

"You should grow them higher up," someone commented.

"Easier pickings for the birds if we do." Gabriella said.

One by one the guest tailed off back to coffee and some of Carmel's delicious cake, but Gabriella worked on with the others. It was hard going, but she enjoyed the camaraderie of friends and neighbours who came to help, most of whom she had known since childhood, so it was a chance to catch up on the local gossip.

One young man, Filipo, from the nearby village, had long ago asked her out and she had spent a few evenings with him, but sadly he wasn't her type and she'd had to let him down gently. She found him working alongside her and could see by his eager expression that he was as keen as ever. She was polite but noncommittal, answering his questions about her time in London.

The buckets were filled at last and they all moved to the shed, following the loaded tractor. The grapes were tipped into the crusher to remove the stems and the juice began to run. It was always an exciting moment at the thought of the new wine to come and Gabriella's heart lifted at the sight. She knew Antonio had high hopes for this year's harvest because the weather conditions had been perfect. The juice was put into oak barrels and yeast added to the fermentation process. She knew some vineyards use steel vats, but Antonio firmly believed the ancient oak barrels improved the flavour of the wine.

Later it would be racked, which meant clearing out any impurities; then finally, some weeks hence, it would be bottled and labelled with the Castello crest. A few of the guests had trailed back to see what was happening and cups of fresh juice were handed round. Antonio explained, through Gabriella, that wine making had started over 4000 years before and it was the Romans who had introduced barrels. Wine, to them, was a daily necessity. "Hear, hear." muttered one of the guests.

"It was made in wine boxes called gondolas."

"I thought they were boats in Venice" someone else remarked.

"Yes, that too. The wine," Gabriella continued, translating Antonio's words, "depends on the type of soil, the weather, the air quality and the amount of sunlight the grapes get. Italy is the biggest wine producer of all and has the biggest number of wine drinkers."

They all laughed and someone said, "Cheers to that!"

"And did you know that the city of Pompeii was the epicentre for wine making in ancient Rome? The Pompeians worshipped Bacchus, the god of wine. The eruption of Vesuvius destroyed all the vineyards of course." She was still speaking when there was a disturbance outside the shed.

It was Josh and Lucia bringing very welcome food for the hungry workers. He and Lucia spread the boxes and packages out over the tables under the shade of the nearby trees. Gabriella thought that sometimes people volunteered to help with the vendemmia because they knew they would be rewarded with a groaning feast at the end of it. Although farmers on the whole ate well, those that worked for them often earned very little money and, as she had explained to some of the guests when they had requested typical Tuscan dishes, they were surprised to be told about dishes that didn't contain expensive meat; the so-called Cucina Povera, poor man's kitchen, ironically now becoming fashionable, but often the staple diet for those who couldn't afford expensive food.

Now, of course, she had given instructions that the table should be groaning with salami, ham, duck, chicken and cheeses of all descriptions, and she stood and watched in satisfaction as the workers of the morning set to demolish the lot washed down with liberal amounts of last year's vintage.

Filippo hung back, waiting for her to sit down, which she finally did after waiting for all the others to have their pick of the delicacies. He made sure he was sitting next to her, moving as close to her as he could.

Gabriella had a naughty thought. She felt guilty about playing Filippo along, but she knew Josh was watching as he waited with Lucia to clear away afterwards, and she leaned towards Filippo who, feeling himself encouraged, put his arm around her.

She didn't resist but turned to him, laughing vivaciously as if finding him the most interesting man on the planet.

Josh moved around the table, collecting the empty dishes. At one point, he was right opposite her and she looked up and met his gaze. He smiled down and she knew instantly that he understood what she was up to. He could obviously read her mind only too well.

"Touche," he mouthed.

She grinned in reply.

Their gaze held and it seemed for a moment that the world around them had disappeared and it was only the pair of them alone together.

Chapter 43

Lupo was missing.

Normally, when there were no guests in the hotel, he followed her around like a shadow, always one step behind her; occasionally touching the back of her knee with his nose as if to reassure her he was always there for her. He still slept in her room all the time, curled up by the side of her bed, the last thing she saw at night, the first thing she saw when she opened her eyes in the morning.

She went into the kitchen, where of course he wouldn't be allowed to go anyway but she asked Carmela and Lucia if they had seen him.

No, they hadn't.

Tommaso was outside cleaning the minivan but he hadn't seen him either. Neither had Antonio, busy in his office with orders.

She began to worry. Worry turned to panic.

Always at the back of her mind was the thought of Domenico. Was he mad enough to kidnap her dog? Surely not.

She visited her father's grave, thinking he might be there, as the dog came with her every time she herself went and he might be sitting by the graveside.

No Lupo.

She checked the sheds and stables in case he had become locked in by accident.

Finally, after an hour of frantic searching when she was getting more and more hysterical, convinced that the worst had happened, she saw Josh coming up the drive. And behind him, there was Lupo lolloping along behind him safe and sound.

She ran to greet them.

"Where have you been?" She shouted.

"Is everything alright?" Josh said, looking at her anxious face.

"It is now," she said, taking a deep breath and stroking Lupo's head to reassure herself. "I just couldn't find Lupo." She hesitated. "And I had the silliest thought that maybe Domenico might have taken him."

"I'm so sorry," Josh said remorsefully. "It was silly of me. I should have said. It was such a nice morning and I felt like a walk and Lupo followed me. I went down the drive to check the hotel sign was still ok and there was no rubbish near the gates and then, well, I just carried on walking."

"It's alright. No harm done. I'm glad you had a good walk."

"Sorry," he said again. "If I ever find him with me again, I'll let you know."

They went into the Castello by the back door and he bent to take off his muddy boots. Gabriella took up the old towel she used to clean Lupo's paws and he sat, obediently lifting one paw after another to be wiped free of mud.

Then, as Josh put on a clean pair of shoes and stood up, Gabriella watched as Lupo went towards him and sat by him before rising and following him back into the main hall.

She didn't know whether to laugh or cry. Lupo had made his decision.

He had a new master now.

****

But Antonio's work wasn't yet finished. After the grapes came the olives. Two hundred trees, some of them thousands of years old, lay in the valley of the estate which Antonio had been carefully curating the whole year, pruning them after the first frosts, checking them regularly for a fruit fly infestation or the dreaded Xylella, the bacteria which had so devastated the olive trees in Puglia in the heel of the country. Luckily all the trees were pronounced healthy and the army of workers and volunteers were ready and waiting as they began. Again, some of the guests had also expressed an interest in helping and Antonio was dubious, worried that they would just get in the way but they proved surprisingly helpful, coming down dressed in jeans and casual shirts, ready to muck in.

One of the female guests was in a smart pair of trousers and Gabriella looked at her dubiously.

"You will spoil those. I could lend you an old pair if you like."

"My dear," laughed the woman, "that's a very kind thought but they would never fit me. You have a much better figure than I do. Don't you think so?" She was looking at Josh who was obviously embarrassed but nodded politely.

She then made it worse by commenting again, loudly, "Oh, I think he has. I can see by his expression."

Gabriella had of course been helping since she was a child so she was able to explain the procedure.

"Like grapes for wine, the olives have to be picked and pressed the same day so no precious oil is lost. On average, there are about 1,000 olives on each tree." They were helping spread the nets in a wide area, having first cleared the ground of weeds so the surface was smooth. The ladders were placed against the tree and a long-handled vibrating tong shook the branches until the fruit rained down. They gathered it up quickly and it was transported to the press. They varied in colour from green which were just ripe fruits to black which were very ripe. Some were kept separate so Carmela could stuff them with pimentos and pickle them for eating.

One of the guests bit into an olive. "Ugh," he said, "that's horrible." He spat it out.

"You should have asked me," laughed Gabriella. " I could have warned you how bitter they are before they are pickled."

"Well, now I know," he said cheerfully. "I will have to be patient." They watched as the olives were crushed and pressed, marvelling at the flood of pure rich green olive oil that came from the pressing machine, the extra, extra, virgin oil. Then it was bottled and the guests helped apply the labels bearing the Castello crest. "Wow, that was fun," they said. "But we're ready for a long soak in the bath and a good dinner." Which they got of course because autumn was the time to harvest all manner of good things.

Carmela had made bruschetta, slices of toasted bread spread with minced roast chestnut, fresh from the trees and mixed with the new oil; pumpkin ravioli, wild boar sauce, and truffle risotto, for it was the time of plenty. To accompany the feast was the delight of Carmela's delicious homemade bread, warm from the oven and dipped in the fresh oil straight from the tree. "This is heaven," the guests said. "We could happily subsist on bread and wine if it was all as good as this." Gabriella helped when she could over the few weeks it took to bring the olive harvest in and Josh too when things were quieter in the hotel and they often found themselves working side by side in companionable silence. Occasionally, their fingers would brush when they reached for the same box of olives and Gabriella noticed he no longer hastily withdrew his hands when his fingers touched hers. And of course when everyone had their olive harvest in and the oil made there would be competitive oil tastings between the neighbours, just as wine tastings are held, and vociferous arguments as to whose was the best.

Chapter 44

They loved the Castello of course. Josh's parents arrived at the front door with Paola and Renato. They got out of the car and stood looking at the view.

"This is breathtaking," Josh's mother said as she gazed up at the ancient sandstone walls and the crenelated towers, then turned to look at the panorama of the valley and the whole estate spread out before her. "And all this is yours?"

"Yes, I'm afraid so?" She almost felt guilty.

"What a responsibility," Josh's father whistled. "I can see why you need help." They went inside and she introduced them to Carmela and Antonio who were in the kitchen. Antonio was having a coffee break, sitting at the table where his wife was preparing some lamb for their lunch, the herbs laid out in bunches, rosemary, oregano and tarragon freshly picked from the herb bed outside the kitchen door. Antonio sprang to his feet and Carmela wiped her hands on her apron as the party came in and Gabriella introduced them.

"This is my right-hand man and my right-hand woman," she laughed. "I couldn't do without them. They have almost brought me up single-handed. Antonio looks after the estate and you will sample some of Carmela's delicious cooking at lunchtime." Carmela coloured up at the praise. They moved on round the Castello. She showed them the antique tapestries on the wall and the portraits of her ancestors. They grew quieter and quieter at each revelation of her wealth and privilege and she was beginning to feel uneasy. She was yet again reinforcing Josh's opinion that she far outclassed him.

Then Josh's father surprised her by saying, "Some people might envy you having all this but I can see what a huge burden your father left you. You are very courageous to have taken it on and done what you have done."

"Thank you but I'm not at all courageous. I just found the best way to deal with the problem. We live in the modern world where wealth and privilege are sometimes not easy to deal with and I could wish sometimes that I could have returned to live the simple life of a student, but fate left me this so I have to get on with it." It was a relief to know that Josh's father at least and maybe the others too, rather than envying her, actually felt sorry for her. She was aware of Josh, standing beside his family, listening to the conversation and she hoped he was taking in what was being said and remembering that moment of recognition on the train when he was looking at a student, a mere girl, not a Contessa with a castle. Just a man looking at a woman. There was a silence and then she said, "Shall we sit on the terrace, have a drink and admire the view?" Which is exactly what they did.

They sat and chatted, drinking Prosecco until Lucia came and called them into lunch which started with cured ham from one of the local farms, together with fresh ripe figs and bread made by Lucia that morning. Then there was a small bowl of freshly made pasta dressed with wild boar sauce, and while they ate, they talked about life in England. Josh's mother mentioned how hard it had been to adjust but now, of course, with a quick glance at her husband and a smile, she was very happy. They moved on to language difficulties and Gabriella had them all in hysterics by repeating the conversation she had had with Josh about the time the man who mangled Italian had called her a sederino, a little bottom, instead of a signorina. There was further hilarity when she told them about the occasion when an elderly Englishman had asked her if it was possible for her to give him a little nookie. She was just about to call Josh and have him ejected when, just in time she realised that what he was actually asking for was some gnocchi.

The next course was the lamb that they had seen being prepared that morning, followed by Carmela's delicious homemade gelato. And then petit fours and liqueur made of tiny strawberries grown in their own vegetable garden.

"Whew, that was some meal," Josh's dad leaned back in his chair. "I think I need a walk."

So after their coffee, they took a stroll around the garden and the fields and Gabriella even introduced them to Tosca.

"What a lovely horse," said Paola stroking her flank. "I didn't realise you rode."

"Gabriella is hoping to ride in the joust in Arezzo," Josh said.

"What, the famous Joust of the Saracen? I didn't know they allowed women to ride in it?"

"They don't but she's hoping to change their minds," Josh said grinning at her.

"Well, good for you," Paola said in admiration. "I hope you succeed."

The guests departed at last amidst much hugging and kissing, having had a wonderful day.

"Please come again to see us soon," were Paola's parting words.

"I hope to," Gabriella replied.

"Thank you," Josh said as they watched the car disappear down the long drive. "Thank you for giving them such a splendid day. I could see they really enjoyed it."

"My pleasure. They are all lovely people." Gabriella smiled at him before she turned and went into the kitchen to thank Carmela and Lucia for a lovely lunch and tell them how much everyone had enjoyed it.

Chapter 45

It was 2 am when she was awoken by frantic pounding on her bedroom door. She leapt out of bed and threw open the door. It was Antonio. "There is a fire in the stable," he shouted. "I've called the brigade but we need to get Tosca out." Full of dread, Gabriella threw on a jacket over her nightdress and a pair of shoes and raced down the stairs after him. Carmela was outside in her dressing gown.

"She's ok for now," she assured Gabriella, "It's in the empty block next door."

"I'll go in," Antonio shouted but Gabriella was already ahead of him, holding the sides of her jacket up against her mouth and nose to shield her from the acrid smoke. Head down, she went through the door, terrified at what she would find, that Tosca would have already been overwhelmed by smoke. Tosca was alright but moving restlessly around in the stable whinnying frantically as Gabriella slammed open the door, grabbed a halter and placed it quickly around the mare's neck.

"Come on, Tosca, we need to go," she said soothingly, trying not to further panic the horse. By now, flames were crackling through the corridor of the next-door stable and it became increasingly urgent that they got out before Tosca's stable was on fire with the horse and herself inside. For a moment, the billowing smoke obscured the walls and she didn't know where she was. She wasn't even sure she was going in the right direction. Was she going towards the fire or away from it? She had a moment of sheer terror when she thought they were both going to perish in the flames. Then she realised there was a window on her right and she suddenly got her bearings. She pushed on feeling her way along the wall until she felt air on her face. Luckily, the girl and horse had the closest of bonds and by dint of coaxing and pulling, she managed to lead the horse out through the choking fumes.

When they emerged, Gabriella, her eyes half closed with the effect of the smoke, suddenly found herself the subject of an enormous embrace and it took few moments for her to realise who it was. "Oh god, Gabriella. Oh, my darling. I thought I'd lost you." It was Josh. She let go of the horse's halter and Antonio caught it and led Tosca away before handing the reins to Carmela while he returned to battle the flames. Others were there too and she could dimly see them through her half-open eyes. All was noise and confusion and an intense heat. But now all her attention was on Josh. His face was a blur but she could feel his arms around her and that was all that mattered. Despite the danger she had been in she was deliriously happy.

Then she could only whisper hoarsely, "Tosca?"

"She's fine," Carmela said. Josh released her at last to go and help put out the flames and Carmela led her away to sit down on a bench. She went to fetch a bowl filled with water and tenderly washed some of the grime from Gabriella's face. The fire brigade arrived with clanging bells and the fire was finally doused though the stables were smouldering ruins and looking at them Gabriella realised with a shudder how very near she had come to death." But how?" Gabriella said, "How did it start?"

"We don't know," Carmela said. "It was fortunate that our cottage is so near the stables. All I know is that I woke up because there were some noises. A car drawing up down on the driveway, the sound of footsteps. I got up and looked out. I could see someone creeping round outside but I couldn't make out who it was. Then I saw the flames and woke Antonio. Whoever it was had gone. The car wasn't there anymore." A nasty suspicion had formed in Gabriella's mind. Was Domenico mad enough to try such a thing? Who else was vengeful enough? He knew she loved her horse so that would be his way of getting back at her for all those imagined slights.

The fire chief came up to her and explained. "We have to do further tests but it does seem to have been arson."

What seemed like hours later they went into the kitchen where Carmela made hot drinks for them all. Josh was sitting very near her, watching her anxiously. Her jacket smelled of smoke and there was a scorch mark on one side showing how near she had come to the flames. She was still coughing from the smoke she had inhaled. Antonio had settled Tosca down and let her out in the field, making sure first of all that she was completely unharmed. Gabriella could feel the pressure of Josh's shoulder against her. It wasn't a cold night but she began to shiver, a reaction from the shock.

"I think you need to get back to bed," Carmela said in concern. "We can sort out the damage in the morning. Luckily, it wasn't the Castello and luckily we had no one staying."

"I will take her up," Josh said firmly and Gabriella's eyes had cleared enough for her to see the amused look that passed between Carmela and Antonio. Josh led her carefully up the stairs and opened her bedroom door. "Is it alright if I come in?" She turned to him and despite the overwhelming weariness she felt all of a sudden and her dishevelled state she smiled weakly at him.

"I would be very unhappy if you didn't."

"I have been such a fool," he said, once they were inside. "I should have followed my first instincts and not been so proud. From the moment I saw you, I was in love. I didn't think it was possible for it to happen like that. It has been agony trying to resist touching you every time I saw you."

"Me too," she replied happily. He held her close and kissed her.

" Ah," he said. "That wasn't how I first imagined kissing you properly. There was a lot of grit."

Gabriella laughed. "I look forward to a better one later but now I need to clean my face again and get rid of this jacket." He led her into the bathroom and tenderly helped her to wash, carefully removing most of the last of the grit and grime. "I will have a proper shower in the morning," she said. Then she added, "Come here." She led him to the narrow bed and they both climbed in. He turned his face to her and kissed her again.

"Better," he said, "and maybe one more just to make sure. Mm," he said, "I think this experiment could go on all night but you are tired and shocked. That is enough for now." And they fell asleep together, arms entwined around each other until dawn broke and she awoke smiling happily as she looked at his sleeping face and knew everything was going to be alright from now on.

Chapter 46

They caught Domenico and there was enough forensic evidence to charge him. Confident that he wouldn't be caught, in his stupidity, he had merely stuffed his clothing in the back of the wardrobe and the carabinieri soon found it as they searched his house. The smell of smoke mingled with petrol made it quite obvious that he was the culprit.

Gabriella who had led the police there, watched as they cuffed him. Domenico glared at her, a look of such hatred that she shuddered.

"I'll get you one day. Be sure that I will," he screamed. "It all should have been mine, mine, not left to some scrap of a girl who doesn't know what she's doing."

In a strange way, she almost felt sorry for him and she certainly felt sorry for Cara who looked small and diminished watching her son being led away to a prison cell. And, even odder, she felt in some strange way that he had done her a favour. If he hadn't set the fire and if she hadn't had to go into the stable to rescue Tosca, she might never have found out how Josh felt about her. Carmela and Antonio smiled every time they saw the pair of them together, holding hands and kissing when they thought no one was looking. "At last!" Carmela said, "We could see you were made for each other from the moment he came here."

"It is just like your mother and father all over again," Antonio said. "There was such electricity between them, you could have used it for the national grid."

Gabriella went about all the usual hotel tasks, singing to herself and laughing over the silliest things she was so happy. Josh had also accepted her offer of becoming a partner in the hotel. "I would be very honoured," he said simply and they had sealed the pact with another kiss of course.

****

Business was brisk in the days leading up to the joust and she had arranged her usual trip for the guests, with lunch in the apartment at the palazzo. overlooking the square. Then, four days before the joust the phone rang. Gabriella answered with a cheerful. "Castello Hotel."

A voice came on the line and her heart jumped. It was the Rettore. "Gabriella," he began, "have you been practising?"

"Yes," she said, excitement beginning to rise in her. "Why?"

"We have a problem," he continued. "Luca, one of our riders, has had a car accident."

"Oh, I am sorry to hear that. Is he badly hurt?"

"No, not too bad, but a broken arm and bad bruising."

"So?" She urged. "He cannot, of course, ride in the joust and our next best rider is unavailable because his father is ill." She waited, impatiently.

"So we were wondering."

"Yes?"

"Would you be willing to ride for us?" Her heart was beating so fast she thought it would burst.

"I think so. I shall have to consult my manager. We have a hotel full of guests, so I am very busy, but I am sure he and the rest of the staff will be able to cope. Can I get back to you in ten minutes?" She flew immediately to Josh and told him the news. "Do you think it will be alright? I mean we are very busy. I can always say no," she said.

"Are you mad!" he grinned. "Of course, you must do it. It's the thing you most want to do in the world, apart from marrying me," he said.

"Oh," she said her heart leaping, "is that a proposal?"

"What do you think?" His expression changed and he was looking at her earnestly now.

"Yes, oh yes," she replied. "And you are right. It's the second thing I most want to do, apart from marrying you." And Carmela, coming out of the kitchen, retreated hastily at the sight of them in the hallway, entwined in a passionate embrace. She shook her head nostalgically remembering how she had felt about Antonio all those years ago and reminding herself how she should tell him she loved him more often. So it took a little longer for Gabriella to return the Rettore's call.

"The answer is yes," she said.

"Good," said the Rettore. "You will have to register yourself and your horse of course."

"Tell me the day and the time and I'll be there." In the meantime, they had to tell the family that they were engaged. Josh's father's reaction was predictable.

"I knew he'd see sense at last." He chuckled.

His mother was ecstatic. "How soon can we come over so I can give you a proper hug?" She said.

"As soon as possible. I hope I will be a good daughter-in-law."

"Cara mia , you have already proved that you are a woman of character. I couldn't ask for a better one."

But the person whose opinion mattered most was of course Paola's.

They drove to Assisi, this time with Josh in the driving seat.

"I'm not sure I'm going to survive married life very long when you are in charge of the car." He teased, then kissed her before firmly taking the wheel.

They leapt out of the car as soon as it stopped at the farm and Paola was running towards them. Gabriella raced towards her and the pair of them hugged, both with tears of joy in their eyes.

"Such wonderful news. I, we are so happy, so very happy for you both. Tell me, have you made plans yet for the wedding?"

"Not really, but it will be soon, as soon as we have time and the hotel is quieter."

"But you have no family to support you."

Gabriella looked at her in astonishment. "Of course, I do. Antonio is to escort me to the church and Carmela and Rosanna will be my matrons of honour."

In fact, she had already asked them the previous evening and their joyful expressions, coupled with the humble pride they felt at the honour said it all. They were her true family, the ones that had cared for her from birth and had guarded her every moment.

Chapter 47

The mortar exploded at 7 am precisely but Gabriella had already been up for several hours. Tosca was groomed and saddled. "This is our big day," Gabriella whispered in Tosca's ear and the horse's ears twitched as if she understood. Gabriella hadn't in fact had much sleep at all; for several days in fact. It had begun when the Rettore had introduced her to her fellow rider Gianfranco. She saw the expression of shock on his face when he had caught sight of her which he couldn't quite conceal. He was polite and outwardly respectful but she could see that privately, he was appalled. There was no warmth behind his eyes as he greeted her. She had the feeling that he considered the joust lost before it had even begun. They must have been really desperate, which was probably what he was thinking if they had actually had to get a woman to ride. It hadn't helped that the Rettore had introduced her as the daughter of his great friend Count Valdarno, the Contessa Gabriella di Valdarno, which made it sound as if there was the whiff of nepotism in allowing her to ride, regardless of her ability.

Even adding the fact that the count had been a five-time champion didn't mean that she herself was a halfway capable rider. She smiled and held out her hand, daring him not to shake it. "Gabriella," she said firmly. "Piacere, pleased to meet you." Things hadn't improved when they began to practise. She missed the target completely on the first run. She could see the contempt in his eyes. Then on the second run, a miracle happened. She scored a five. Things improved rapidly after that and by the time the practice session ended, he was looking much less sceptical but the whole experience made her even more determined to do well. She had never been a shrinking violet and given a challenge she had always risen to it. She would show them if it killed her! Not only was she riding against three other quarters but she even had to prove herself to her own side as the scepticism wasn't over yet.

On the day before the joust, the registration of the jockeys took place in front of the church of San Francesco and a small procession from each quarter joined up in one long line as always and paraded around the city. Eager crowds stood at the side of the road, the tourists and the locals out in force with the town band drumming them to the dais where, one by one, the riders dismounted and led their charges up the steps and to the table where their names would be inscribed for posterity.

It was a solemn and unique moment. Gabriella felt the weight of history on her shoulders. Tosca behaved impeccably as horse and rider were registered and Gabriella was sure the horse was enjoying the whole thing even more than she was, tossing her head so her mane flew in skittish fashion. There was a moment's hesitation when she gave her name as the official was sure he hadn't heard correctly and he looked up in astonishment. She smiled sweetly in return. Most people hadn't noticed she was a woman because her hair was up under her helmet and the costume concealed her shape. The street party for the quarter was held that night and she was sitting at the top table with the Rettore and his committee. There had been a gasp from some of the supporters who hadn't already heard the news when she took her place and was introduced as one of the riders for the joust the next day. She could hear the buzz of comments from the people near her. Many of the men were outraged and said they were resigned to losing that year if they were so desperate as to allow a woman to ride.

But the women were cheering that at last the barrier of male riders only had been broken. Furious arguments were breaking out all over the place between husbands and wives, boyfriends and girlfriends. She only hoped she wouldn't let down the ones who supported her. She was striking a blow for women everywhere. The guests from the hotel had been astonished too to find out that the owner of the hotel was actually going to ride in the joust. She had to explain to those people who thought she would be accompanying them that she was deputising Antonio to explain the intricacies of the rules to them, with Josh translating. A few people actually came up to take selfies with her and she had to remind herself that it was a serious business and that she wasn't just some visiting film star.

She had gone to bed the previous night in the palazzo in the square but had had very little sleep, tossing and turning and obsessing over the day ahead. Now she stood on the balcony with her morning coffee looking out at the empty square, newly arrayed with ranks of metal seats for the spectators. She gazed down at the diagonal strip of sand that ran from the bottom left-hand corner near the old well to the top right-hand corner of Vasari's loggia where it met the

Tribunale. She had already galloped up there a few times in the last few days. The last time had been in the Prova, the final rehearsal two days ago. Santa Crucifera had come third of the four quarters when she herself had scored a three. But then so had Gianfranco, so she felt she had acquitted herself reasonably well. 'Must do better, must do better,' she muttered to herself. And today was the day when it had to happen. Josh of course was in charge of the guests and was bringing them into the city later on to enjoy the spectacle. "In Bocca al Lupo," he had whispered to her when she had left the Castello. " I love you." He kissed her and then he had added with a grin, "Sock it to them. Show them what a woman can do!"

She changed into the costume that had been laid out on one of the spare beds. It had had to be altered especially for her as it had, of course, been made for a man. She squeezed into the tight trousers, one leg red, the other green, a tight-fitting jacket with red epaulettes, a cap with a plume, the colours of Santa Crucifera, the decorated leather boots. She looked at herself in the mirror. "Gabriella," she said firmly to her reflection, "you look amazing." She spent an hour at the local stables where the horses for the joust were securely guarded, getting Tosca ready and having a few practice runs. Then it was time to go and prove to the world that she really could do it

Chapter 48

When the 11 am mortar sounded, she and Tosca, together with Gianfranco and his horse, were at the church with a small entourage. They dismounted and Gabriella led Tosca up the dimly lit aisle towards the altar where she and Gianfranco knelt, heads bowed to be blessed by the priest. She couldn't help remembering the times when, as a young child, she had watched her father being blessed in the same way. She felt the deep significance of the moment and then, raising her head, she saw the priest looking down at her and smiling in encouragement. He then turned to the horses and Gabriella was touched to see Tosca bending her head as she was blessed as if she too was aware of the importance of the occasion.

Then they were out in the bright sunshine again and on their way to the square. It was really happening. Today was the day when she had to prove herself to the world.

****

To say she was nervous was an understatement. She and the other riders were assembled outside the square while the parade took place. They could hear the drumming, the call of the bugles, then they had to wait while the rest of the participants filed past; the captains of each quarter, their entourage, the lancers, the crossbowmen, then the bandieri, the flag throwers ,going through their routine. The wait seemed endless and to make it worse she would be the last of the eight to ride. The supporters in the square, corralled in each of their separate corners, screamed insults or encouragement depending on their quarter. Tosca was behaving well considering the noise. Gabriella patted her neck and spoke to her soothingly.

Then suddenly it was serious. The mood in the square changed. There was a tense silence, then a roar, as the first rider went through the gates, from Porta del

Foro, the pink and gold. She heard the Master of the Field, the Maestro del Campo, announce him, the seemingly endless wait for the lance to be brought down by an attendant on horseback, then there was the sound of the galloping horse and the bang as his lance hit the target. Gabriella and the other riders listened attentively. There had been a roar from a section of the crowd who could see the target so they knew the rider had done well: but how well? There was an agonising wait as the target was taken down and rushed to the waiting judges. The result was taken to the Maestro del Campo and the assembled crowd held its breath. In true theatrical fashion, the Maestro read out the result. " The first rider from the quarter Porto del Foro has scored," he then paused dramatically, "four points." There were wild cheers and an equal number of boos.

Then it was the turn of the first rider from Porto Santo Spirito, the blues and yellows. He galloped; there was a bang and a collective groan. He had only scored two. Then Sant'Andrea, the green and white, was next. He also scored a three. Then it was time for the first rider from her quarter, Gianfranco, to go. Gabriella watched as the gates opened and he went through. The long pause was agonising. At last, she heard the sound of him galloping up the sand and the bang as he hit the target. There was a babble of noise from the supporters who obviously couldn't see the target. She waited anxiously for the result.

He had scored a four. There were screams of joy. Tosca was getting restive, wheeling in circles. She was raring to go and Gabriella fought to calm her. Still the wait went on. It was now the turn of the second riders. The second rider from Porto del Foro also scored four which meant she had to score at least a four to force a second round. Santo Spirito and Sant'Andrea both only scored twos so they were already out of the competition. Then at last, at last, it was her turn. The huge gates opened in front of her and she was in the square. The sight of all that massed crowd of spectators was unnerving but she had quelled the sudden feeling of panic and shut her mind to them. She had a job to do. Somewhere above her Josh was sitting on the balcony with all the hotel guests but she dared not look up. She waited patiently as the attendant on the horse came plodding down the sand strip towards her bearing the lance. "This is for you, Papa. Give me your strength and your resilience," she murmured. She took the lance and bent to whisper in Tosca's ear, "Come on, Tosca, we can do it." She wheeled her around and faced the target.

She flew up the sand and the tip of the lance hit the target.

The wait was agonising.

She had scored a four and the crowd went wild. It meant that Porta Crucifera, her quarter and Porto del Foro had made equal scores of eight. Therefore the two riders on each side had to go again to decide the winner. The four riders gathered once again outside the starting gate. Gianfranco was looking as tense as she felt but at least he did look at her and force a smile of encouragement. The first rider from Porto del Foro went through the gates again. There was the inevitable wait for the lance to be brought down, then the sound of galloping and the final bang. Screams of joy erupted around the stadium when the result was announced. He had scored a four. It was Gianfranco's turn. He made the sign of the cross and started his run. He only scored a three. Their supporters groaned in despair. Then the second rider from Porto del Foro scored a five and the crowd screamed. They had won. The supporters went mad. It was all over. Even if Gabriella scored a five she couldn't win.

There was, however, just the faintest of chances. She remembered as a small girl what had happened once when her father had won the Golden Lance against all odds and she knew the rules, one obscure one in particular. She whispered in Tosca's ear and Tosca responded. They flew at a fast gallop up the strip of sand and Gabriella concentrated as she had never concentrated before in all her life. The point of the lance hit the target and the Buratto swung around, metal balls flying on their chains. She felt the force of the impact as if her arm joint had disconnected, it was so hard.

And the lance broke.

For a second, there was a deadly silence. Then those who didn't know what it signified groaned in despair.

But for those who did know its meaning, it was a moment of pure unadulterated joy. She had scored a four but ,according to the ancient rules of the joust, the breaking of the lance doubled the points. She had ensured victory for her side with a total of eleven points over Porto del Foro's nine. They were galloping so fast that she was well round the corner before Tosca finally came to a halt and Antonio was there to catch Tosca's reins as Gabriella slid from the saddle to the ground. Tears were streaming down his face. He was sobbing with joy.

"Gabriella, you are a miracle. Your father would have been so proud, so very, very proud. And I am so very proud too." He hugged her but she was already surrounded by an exuberant crowd of supporters who had broken ranks and come surging forward. A few moments later, the result was officially confirmed and she was lifted high on the shoulders of the supporters and carried through the square. The people in the stands were on their feet applauding and cheering. Among them she could see Paola and Renato who had come especially to support her. Despite the mass of people, she was able to look up at the balcony and there was Josh waving and cheering wildly with all the guests surrounding him. She longed to be with him but now was not the moment. Holding her trophy, the Golden Lance, she was swept along on a tide of humanity up the hill to the cathedral where the bishop was waiting. And there was Antonio with Tosca and horse and rider entered the cathedral together with Gianfranco and his mount to give thanks for their victory, "Well ridden" he said and there was a new respect in his eyes.

The Rettore and all his committee were there too to congratulate them. The drummers were already preparing for the victory parade and they were marched round the city surrounded by ecstatic supporters. It was a long night as she fielded congratulations from everyone, including a few of the committee who had been set against her. She received their congratulations modestly though she was longing to say, "So you see, a woman can do it after all!" At long last, she was able to slip away and Antonio drove her, together with Tosca in the horse box, back to the Castello. And there was Josh, waiting impatiently for her on the steps.

"I will see to Tosca," Antonio said quickly and she thanked him gratefully as she gave Tosca a final pat before she was led away, whispering, "Thank you." And Tosca's ears twitched in response.

"You were so wonderful, you are so wonderful," Josh said, sweeping her into his arms.

And as they walked together in the small hours of the night under a starlit sky she said, "You know in English heraldry, the knight who wins is allowed to claim his fair lady. Do you think it works in reverse? Can I claim you as my prize?"

"No," said Josh firmly, just before he took her in his arms, "if there is any claiming to be done, it will be completely on my side."